SIRENS

Tales of Youth and Love

Leroy Mthulisi Ndlovu

Cover art by: Daniel Rodrigues

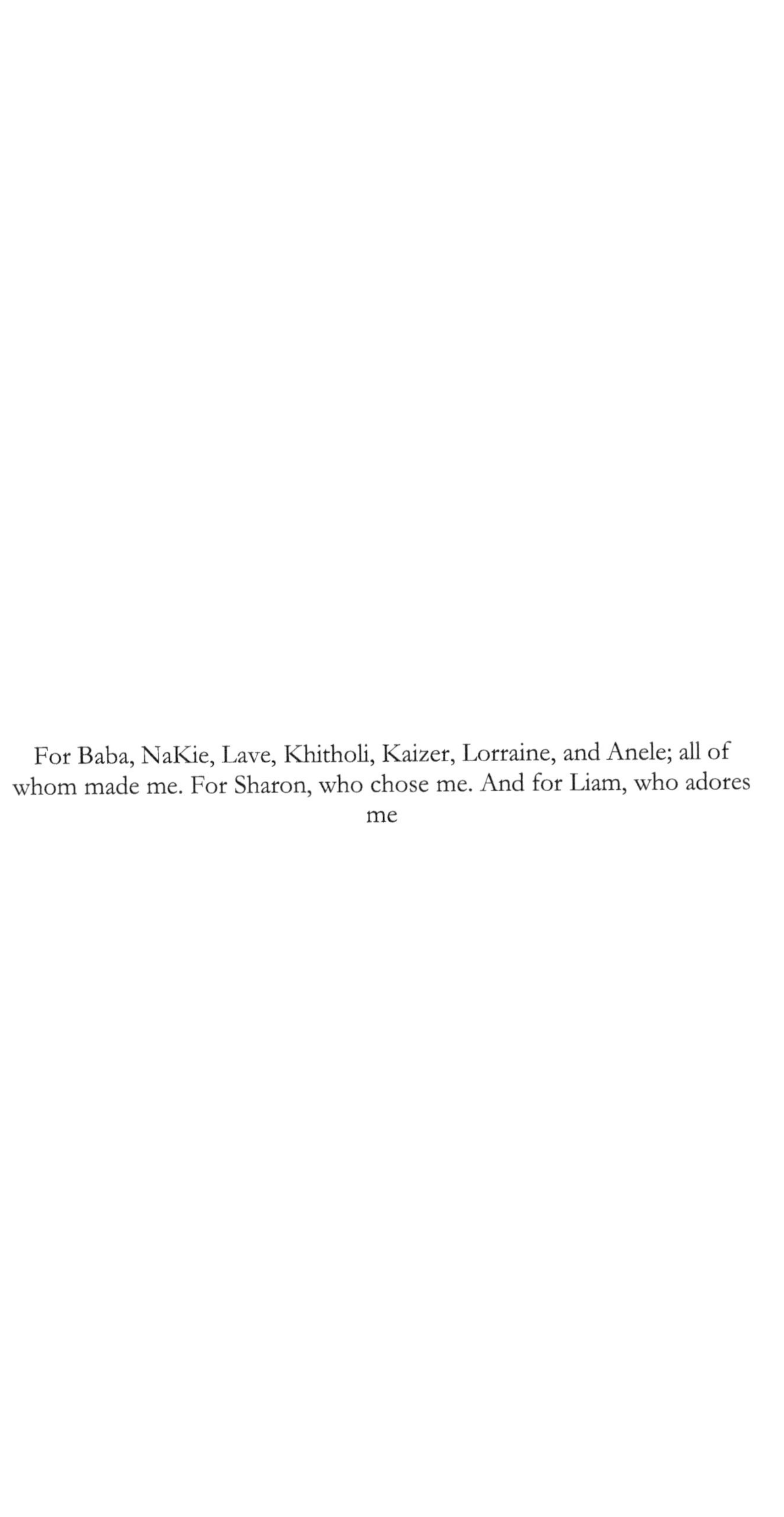

For Baba, NaKie, Lave, Khitholi, Kaizer, Lorraine, and Anele; all of whom made me. For Sharon, who chose me. And for Liam, who adores me

CONTENTS

FOREWORD

Among the literati, it is common to ask if writers are born or made. This is often accompanied by the Shakespeare quote, "some are born great, some achieve greatness, and some have greatness thrust upon them".

This is the question of talent. Are we born with the innate ability to put one word in front of the other coherently, meaningfully, and carry a story to a satisfying (or disturbing) end?

There is a story Leroy tells often; stop me if you know this one. In his fourth form at Christian Brothers' College, he had the distinguished honour of studying Literature in English under John Eppel. During consultation Eppel made a declaration: Leroy is a fine writer. Then came the prophecy: regrettably people like him, proficient in sciences and mathematics tend to gravitate towards the Sciences in their A Levels. I on the other hand made up my mind to take this sodden path early and went to study Arts at A Level but there was stigma attached to our class. This is not to say I had it figured out, I moved as close as I could to writing but have also had other careers to make ends meet. Young people have been taught to play it safe; they are expected to know what they want to do with the rest of their lives and as early as fifteen, to choose a path that leads them in a particular direction; a direction they are expected to take for the rest of their lives. Leroy chose Sciences as Eppel predicted, and would later become a fine computer scientist.

John had given a piece of advice though; whatever path he took, Leroy shouldn't forget his writing pen. It's not a bad thing that he chose a career that would help him put bread on the table; I'm sure Charles Bukowski would have preferred a career in computer science to being a post office worker or a factotum. There are a lot of experiences to be gained from that choice, and perspective that becomes valuable to a publication. And there is a greatly transferrable skill from computer programming to literature: writing code requires one to be fucking meticulous, so does writing. With all the wonders of technology he interacts with daily, Leroy chooses to do his initial writing on Notepad. No red lines on his typos, no blue lines for grammatical errors, just the good old writer and page like good old pen and paper.

I'm not saying beware of being programmed, but here's another story before the foreword turns into a short story on its own. Between 2012 and 2014 we were fine gentlemen, spry of foot and blindly ambitious. I think we still are. Leroy and I, among other writers, contributed to the short story section in The Sunday News. If you ever wanted to write fiction when we were boys, that column was on your bucket-list. And we made it in! I admired his prose, I still do. He writes with a pen, I write with crayons. One of his first publications in the paper was a fine story you will find here, about a guy named Victor who ponders terrible things when horrible things happen to him. The story has only grown better with every consecutive edit of the meticulous author's pen; but that draft, published eight years ago, was so good not one but several people reached out to Leroy, convinced he was the persona, with advice on how to deal with his pain and suffering, hoping to steer him away from what he was contemplating. Damn, now that's writing.

Philani A. Nyoni
Bulawayo
September, 2020

VICTOR'S SONG

Stanza 1: Birth

The midday bus dropped my mother off at the clinic. She'd gone into labour that morning soon after breakfast. At first, she ignored the burgeoning pain in her lower abdomen. There had been a few false alarms before, and this too would pass. Besides, she thought, her father was at work and there was no one to get her to the hospital.

Barely an hour later, she was on the midday bus en-route to Tshabalala Clinic with her little blue preparation bag. In it were her nightgown and a change of clothes, along with some clothes for the baby. It would've been difficult for anyone to guess that the young woman was in labour. My mother was as stubborn as they came, and this being what she thought was a false alarm, she wouldn't call a taxi or an ambulance. She walked, as calmly as she could, into the clinic and sat down in one of the visitor's chairs in the matron's office. The chubby old matron ambled into the room and smiled broadly. A cute smile. Something that made my mother think of a baby inspecting a new object. She stifled a giggle at the image of the old woman's cheeks being pinched.

"So, the day has come, has it?" she asked.

"Probably not," my mother replied, "But I'll feel better if you check anyway."

It wasn't a false alarm.

The matron quickly checked her in and gave her a room where she could wait for my much-anticipated arrival. It was small and cosy. There were no visitor's chairs, only beds, cupboards and a scale. She wondered how many human beings had arrived in this very bed.

The matron's assistant came to keep her company. The scrawny assistant smiled pleasantly beneath her enormous glasses. They'd developed something of a relationship during my mother's monthly check-ups. She offered my mother tea. My mother refused and asked instead for a cup of hot water. While she was fetching it, my mother began to scream, wondering how she could have believed this was a false alarm. And then the matron was in the room. She was stern, but kind, and she remained calm despite my mother's growing hysteria.

"Save your energy," she crooned, "This screaming will only make it harder than it has to be."

The pain was unbelievable. As she lay on the bed waiting to bring me forth my mother vowed never to have another child. It was a big decision for a sixteen-year-old, but it was one she didn't go back on. All the same she held the screams in, only releasing a grunt here and there that she could not trap behind her throat.

An hour passed.

Then the matron told her to get ready. The baby was coming. The assistant stood behind my mother and helped her to push. The matron stood between her legs, waiting to receive the precious cargo. The vice grip on my mother's lower body did not let up. With each push she felt her pelvic bones threatening to break. The room was alive with the sounds of her groans and half screams, and of the matron encouraging her to push

("we're almost there my dear")

one last time so she could see her baby.

At last I emerged, kicking and screaming, out of the darkness. I wept and the world rejoiced. Confused and smarting from the sudden rush of air, I was weighed, wiped and swaddled.

"Congratulations!" The matron cried as she placed me in my mother's arms. "It's a big boy! All of three kilograms!"

My mother hugged me for the first time. She cradled me in her loving arms and kissed my face all over. There was no proud father to watch the scene and beam with satisfaction.

But for that day, at least, the old matron nailed the part.

Stanza 2: A Mother's Tale

I lived my mother's memories as if they were my own.

She first told me the story during one of our famous picnics at the Centenary Park Fountain. Back then the work meant more to our local authority than their salaries. The well-groomed grass remained green even through the harshest of winters. Bright flowers flourished and lent the air their nostalgic scent. The fountain in the middle of the park regularly shot a jet of water high into the air, spraying everyone in the vicinity with a cool refreshing mist. My mother loved it. It was a haven for young love. For the young couple it provided a place without the prying eyes of neighbours and relatives. A young man could avoid the catcalls that neighbourhood boys made whenever they spotted a stranger with a girl they knew. The park held a special place in her heart. Even after my father's betrayal. It was her fortress of solitude. He was a poet, and he wrote her letters laced with some of the most beautiful combinations of words I ever laid eyes on.

Youth and the city spared both my parents the horrors of the war. My mother lived with her father. She was born after her parents stopped hoping for children. My grandmother hit what she assumed was menopause and quickly resolved to spend the rest of her days loving God and her man as the bible intended. It turned out later that she was pregnant. It was the best news my grandparents ever received. But childbirth proved too much for Mrs Kumalo's ageing body and she died giving birth to her only child. This didn't take away from my grandfather's love for his daughter. Even in his grief they were quite a pair. As long as he wasn't working, he took her everywhere he went. Sometimes even to the local shebeen. They were inseparable.

At age fifteen my mother got a job at the neighbourhood school. Her Junior Certificate meant she qualified to teach the younger classes and she took to the profession with furious verve. Many people I grew up around were her former students. My father was a student teacher too. He taught English to the same classes she taught Mathematics. Over time their brief morning greetings evolved to brief morning conversations about the headmaster's previous meeting or the next school event. Rumours of their relationship preceded it by far as they grew more acquainted with each other.

He wrote poetry. He wanted to write it professionally. She laughed when he told her that.

"I never heard of anyone who got rich from writing poems," she said, smiling.

They were in the staff room. He'd gobbled down his breakfast and was watching her intently, occasionally sipping his tea.

"You sound just like my father."

His brow darkened and he continued, "He sits in his wheelchair and condemns the idea even when I don't bring it up. I could be bringing him his morning tea and he'll find something nasty to say about the tea *and* my poetry."

Mother always said he looked deeply sad when his father crept into their conversations.

She asked what his mother thought about his poetry.

"I have no idea," he said through a rueful smile. "She disappeared before I could even walk. According to my old man, she wasn't ready to be a mother."

He averted his eyes.

"The neighbourhood rumours say she was a well-known hooker and she moved to Johannesburg soon after I was born. Whatever," he said and then shrugged.

Love blinded my young mother. The more time they spent together the deeper she fell. Their innocent weekend walks through the park soon became a chance to kiss the love of her life and perform frottage whenever they were out of sight. At last, overcome by desire, the wordsmith deflowered my mother one night in a chalet at the caravan park adjacent to The Centenary. The moon was at its fullest and he walked her there under its satisfied smirk.

Nine months after that, I was born.

At the news of my mother's pregnancy my father beat David

Copperfield at his own game. Never to be seen or heard from again. The bastard. As I grew older so did my hatred. I didn't understand how my mother could have been so naive. How she could have been fooled by this man. Yet I owe him my existence. And who can blame a young maiden for the desire to please her first love, the love of her life? All my life I never saw or heard of my mother being with another man. I watched her hold the torch for a man she would never see again.

It tore me apart.

Stanza 3: A Ray of Hope

Love makes people do incredibly stupid things. In high school my best friend, Patrick, wrote an eight-page letter to his ex-girlfriend. They'd broken up and reconciled about a hundred times by then. Patrick said the letter was no plea for them to patch things up again. It was a goodbye note. An ode to all their time together. We were in our final year. They had been doing their dance for a little over three years. Even I could see that he loved her more than anything else in the world, but Patrick felt that their destinies were on diverging paths. He wanted her to know that he would always love her, even if they could never again share the warmth of each other's embrace.

By then my mother and I had moved out of my grandfather's house. She managed to secure a smaller semi-detached house in Old Magwegwe for a steal. The opportunity was too good to resist. It was a two-roomed affair. My mother had her bedroom, and the other room served multiple functions as the kitchen, dining room, living room and my bedroom. Patrick and I stood outside in the shade of a guava tree. Thembi stayed two doors down from my mother's house. We knew she'd be back from school anytime soon. The afternoon sun blazed mercilessly on the neighbourhood. Patrick was restless. He refused to take any sips from the bottle of gin we were supposedly sharing. He sat down. He stood up. He took a step forward. He sat down again.

"Will you just fucking relax?" I yelled, "It's not like you're about to ask her to marry your ass."

Patrick only smiled at me, "Love is a cruel master, homie."

I could only shake my head and take another gulp of the fast sinking gin.

After what felt like a year Thembi turned onto our road and Patrick's breath caught in his throat. You couldn't blame him. Thembi is still one of the most beautiful women I ever met. There she was in her shortened uniform, strolling carefree toward her house. It was a simple green dress, interrupted by thin white vertical stripes. She looked unbelievably beautiful in it even though people called their school *Green Bombers*. At a time when most would have given both arms and maybe a leg for lighter skin, Thembi was more than comfortable in hers. Patrick raved about it. He called her his ebony princess.

She was reading, her dark lips stuck out in a pout of concentration. I never met another person who could walk and read at the same time. More often than not she had some romance nonsense in hand. She didn't see us.

Patrick leapt over the drainage ditch that ran adjacent to the road and strode purposefully toward her. She stopped in the street and looked up. A bright smile erased the pout. Like I said before, they were madly in love. She spared me a brief wave before Patrick was beside her, speaking to her. He always had a way of talking so softly that only the intended hearer would pick up the words. He spoke to her like that. Then the letter passed from his hands to hers. They hugged. After that she walked away briskly, her romance novel promptly forgotten. Whatever Patrick told her that day remains their secret. All he said to me was that it was done and then he proceeded to help me get rid of the remaining gin.

Whatever he said to her though, it worked. They reunited a few weeks later. And then I blinked and they were getting married. I thought it was a mistake. How could a man vow to love the same woman until he died? You didn't know how long it could be before that day finally came. And worse you could end up having to chase around three or four kids for the rest of your life! But I had grown accustomed to all their lovey-dovey shit. In my mind I just had to sit through a couple of hours of it. After that, I would pretend she didn't exist.

I have never been more wrong in my life.

Stanza 4: Nothing to Lose

Patrick began to insinuate himself into my life on the first day of form three. He was a newcomer. He planted himself in the seat next to mine during registration and in every single class after that.

It annoyed me to begin with. At the time I was a confused young man trying to piece together the meaning of his pathetic existence. My only friends were books. Or rather words. I lived off them. They never disappointed me. When given the chance I would sit in a corner by myself, reading until my eyes hurt. I loved words. They took me halfway around the world and deep into the corridors of adult topics forbidden me by my mother. I walked with the prophets and sat with the twelve at the last supper. I conquered the Pepetas with the great Sigidi and marched with Leonidas at Thermopylae. Words were everything to me. I played with some of the neighbourhood kids in my time, especially during my younger days when my mother left me in the care of our neighbour Mrs Nyathi, but I never had a close friend. Not until I met Patrick.

That first day he sat there and greeted me like we were old pals. I wasn't keen on idle conversation, but he was determined to engage me. He pulled out a space case decorated with images of famous cartoon characters and asked if I knew them. I tried to be distant. He kept pushing. He wanted to know where I stayed. I grudgingly told him. He grinned and said he lived near there, if Phumula could be called near. A snort escaped my lips. People often joked it was so far out of town even the donkeys felt at home there. He wore me down. Slowly I grew fascinated by this dark creature that didn't seem to care what people might think of it. And despite my own irritability his stories drew me in.

He didn't always stay in Phumula. His father was a prominent mechanic and had managed to purchase his own flat in town. His mother stayed home and gossiped with the lady from the flat next door when she wasn't cleaning, washing or baking. Back then some of the government schools were still more prestigious than a lot of the private schools. Patrick went to one such primary school in Kumalo. The largest class he remembered carried only twenty-five students. His father was determined to make sure he could be exposed to a broader world than the one he grew up in. Later he would show me his sky-blue shirts with pride as he recounted his stories of how tough you had to be to survive form one at a high school in the same neighbourhood.

His father drank. He was known to disappear from the house on certain nights only to return the next day smelling like he had taken a swim in some crude mix of whiskey and beer. He'd disappeared in much the same way the previous year and never returned. Patrick's eyes shone with tears as he described the flurry of events that came after that.

A policeman showed up at their door. Patrick was sent to his room and minutes later his mother's wailing filled the flat. Aunts and uncles materialised. His paternal grandfather sat him down and told him that he was now the man of the house. He didn't feel like a man yet though, especially when his father's relatives began looting the place after the funeral. Not even his Nintendo survived the frantic scramble for his father's possessions. When they thought it couldn't get worse his father's older brother moved in with his wife and children. He declared that Patrick's mother was also his wife and he had to make sure she was taken care of. She would have none of it. A week later she moved back to her mother's house in Phumula. Patrick was transferred from what he called the toughest school in the world on the other side of the city to slum it with the rest of us in the high-density suburbs.

Patrick was less concerned with the worlds one could explore in books and TV. He was determined to experience everything he could and slowly over the years he brought me out of my shell. Within months our friendship had grown beyond the confines of the school fence. We became the best of friends.

"Don't you ever get tired of hanging out with each other?" Mother would ask sometimes.

We would walk to my house after school and I would change out of my uniform, and then walk to Patrick's house so he could do the same. Then after that we would walk all the way back to Old

Magwegwe to hang out. He loved my neighbourhood the way a man loves any world he can't quite become a part of. He told me one day that he had never seen so many people living together in such small spaces. Mother and I were by far the smallest family on the block. To our left lived a mixed family of cousins, brothers, a grandmother and an aunt; about seven people in total. On the right they could have numbered well over ten if they had all lived there at the same time.

Patrick and I spent most afternoons sitting on the edge of the drainage ditch outside my home, watching people and (Patrick) chasing girls. As we got older alcohol would join in the party, followed by cigarettes (which I tried once and didn't care for, but Patrick took to the habit like he had been doing it all his life.) If we had serious money, we moved our little party to the local beerhall.

On one such occasion Patrick suggested I solicit the services of Petition. He had been coming to my neighbourhood for so long he knew everyone. We were nineteen. He was well versed with women and their anatomy and I had barely kissed the ones I dated. He often teased me about my failure to taste the joys that awaited every man between a woman's legs. He showed me many things during the course of our friendship, and according to him there was one more thing I needed to learn.

Petition was the neighbourhood's most notorious hooker. Her patrons were as enthralled by her beauty as they were afraid of her temper. Nobody ever tried to screw her over. Pardon the pun. One poor married guy tried it and she dragged him to his house by his balls to demand her money. He told her he'd left his wallet at home, so she took him to his wallet.

Patrick sat across from me at Marisha beer garden that afternoon and smiled like he had just suggested the sanest thing in the world.

"I always suspected you were nuts," I said, holding my glass close to my lips, "But I'm glad you finally decided to prove it."

He laughed and carried on. Petition was also the most beautiful prostitute you could find in Old Magwegwe and the surrounding neighbourhoods. I couldn't disagree. I thought back to when

Mother and I arrived. Petition had been a pretty, caramel-skin high school girl with the modest suggestion of curves beneath her uniform. She was only a few years older than me. She failed dismally, and her father – who never had any interest in sending a girl to school anyway – wasn't too bothered about finding a plan for his daughter afterwards. She disappeared until her parents died in quick succession. When she returned, she took over the house as if she never left, and the Nyoni house became the biggest brothel in the neighbourhood.

"UMaNyo, bra!" Patrick persisted, "She will take you around the world in sixty seconds, my friend."

He wore the same mischievous look he had when he showed up at my house a few years earlier with the idea to buy some gin at the local shops.

"You have nothing to lose man," he declared, "To her it's just business. It won't matter if you suck! I bet if you tell her you're a virgin she'll go easy on you even."

I wasn't that hard to convince. I was a nineteen-year-old virgin with a libido that was raring to go. I'd been unsuccessful with girls before then and here was Patrick, my only friend and a man I had come to consider a brother, offering to facilitate another first for me. He always had access to money, and he paid for my night with Petition. I was a nervous wreck as I prepared to go out. He told me again that I had nothing to lose. He walked me to the corner of her block. We would meet later on at Marisha for drinks and all the dirty details.

And so, Petition made me a man. And I drank and talked to Patrick about it later. I was happy to finally have known a woman, albeit a prostitute. And he was happy I was happy.

We were, after all, brothers for life.

Stanza 5: Dive in It

As pathetic as it sounds, the truth is that Patrick was the only friend I had. After he got married, I spent less time at Marisha. It reminded me too much of what I no longer had. For years I'd been going there with Patrick to drink and argue about football matches we didn't really care about.

Books had long lost their appeal. I couldn't even remember when last I had a novel in my hands. The only other friend I could turn to was a bottle of Russian Tsar. We became well acquainted. It was the first drink we dared to taste in our teenage years, and once Patrick was out of the picture, I spent my days chugging it by the mouthful. It was that or gin, depending on how deep I wanted to dive. I've always liked to believe that I was in control at some point. That for a while I avoided drinking at work, but all I can remember is drinking out of a flask in my office whenever I was alone or stepping out of staff meetings to take a swig in the toilet.

The days began to blur together. Eventually I stopped going to work entirely. By then my hair stood out on my head like wild grass in winter. My face was engulfed by my beard and when I spoke to anyone at work I could see the disgust on their face. I helped them get rid of me by hurling all the obscenities I could think of at the line manager one morning after he showed up at my office looking for one stupid file or another. I was over files. I was over work. I was over everything.

I walked out and went straight to the park. I drifted to the fountain. The water was murky green, and stagnant. I drank from my flask and watched the young couples, with their stolen kisses and their heads laid in each other's laps. All I saw were re-enactments of my mother's story. But I sat there drinking and minding my own business. Day after day I sat there. Being out of a job didn't worry me. It just meant longer drinking hours. I had no rent to worry about. I'd moved into my late grandfather's house after he died and left my mother with two fully furnished houses to look after. I was independent. And my fat bank account meant I could still afford a good fuck every other night.

I lost track of my existence. Day and night blended together seamlessly. Only mornings were significant. They were the only moments when I was sober enough to feel the pain of being lonely again. The alcohol helped me cope. It was weird how unbearable being alone had become. It had never bothered me before. But as I tumbled further and further, I also began to think how much of a waste my life had been all along. It was as if I had come to the world to be the poster boy for lonely men with unnervingly close relationships with their mothers.

I drank at the park all day and started fights in dubious bars at night. Being a drunk has its own strange celebrity. Most people knew to avoid me either from previous experience, or because of a whispered warning about the unpleasant-smelling alcoholic who harassed people for looking at him 'the wrong way.' One time I woke up in the alley behind Hustler's Night Club. My wallet and shoes were gone, and my lip looked like it had lost an argument with a couple of fists. Katsande – the barman and a former classmate's brother – said he had seen me the night before being dragged out by a gigantic boor. He doubted the man had a reason to rob me. He was one of those rough government types who were the country's new rich. I chuckled. I didn't need to be told I had blacked out during the fight.

Even I would've mugged a sucker like that.

Stanza 6: Mama Mia!

My mother often tried to get through to me. She had watched my friendship with Patrick grow from the beginning. When I first told her about the annoying new boy in class who wouldn't leave me alone, she said it was cute that I had a new friend. That annoyed me even more.

By the time Patrick got married, mother's health was failing. She'd been diagnosed with heart disease a few years prior and suffered from multiple problems since. She spent a lot of time reminiscing about our lives when it was just us. Before the drinking and the whores.

Before Patrick and his wedding.

In her efforts to cheer me up she would even ask about some of my favourite characters from books I read years before. It made me smile, but I would often return to the bottle as soon as I left her house. It wasn't that I didn't appreciate her companionship. She was, after all, my first friend and my world. She was with me from day one and nothing could take me away from her. But in Patrick I had found the bond of brotherhood that makes men stand up for each other even in the most ridiculous of fights. I had fought several impossible battles with and for the man. Mother tried her best, but I was too torn. And her ill health sent me further down the path to self-destruction. Everything I loved was slipping away.

Despite the pain that was my companion whenever I was sober, I never went to see my mother drunk. I respected her too much. But there were no secrets; she knew what I had become. If you think the world is a small place, try living in the fishpond that we call a high-density suburb.

So sometimes she would sermonise, "You need to stop drinking. Do you have any idea how brilliant you could be if you just focus and stop pining over Patrick like you're some heartbroken teenager?"

She never needed alcohol or rage to be candid. I would nod and say yes in all the right places, pretending to listen while I struggled to ignore the aching inside for my first drink.

Patrick also tried to get through to me. He showed up at my house early one morning demanding to know what the hell was wrong with me. By then even our once-in-a-blue-moon drinks had stopped. I hadn't seen him in months. To be honest it could even have been more than a year. I had no idea who or what I was.

That morning, my rocket had already taken off. I had some leftover gin and a blunt rolled so carelessly anyone could have guessed that I wasn't used to doing it. Patrick didn't even bother to knock. He just burst through the door, his face the image of disgust as he stepped gingerly over the bottles littered on the sitting room floor. I can't remember why, but I offered him my hand and he shook it before launching into his speech. Patrick had never been any good with words; how he once managed to put together eight pages of them for Thembi remains a mystery to me even today.

I listened in amusement as he stammered his concern for me. When he was done, I only stared at him. My buzz was fading and I was at a loss for words. What did he expect me to say? That I missed him? That I had grown an unhealthy addiction to his guidance? That the steaming pile of shit that was my life was getting worse and I couldn't even think of a single way to stop it? I couldn't. There was no doubt that he was like a hero to me; the big brother I never had. I couldn't tell him, but he knew. Patrick could always tell what I was thinking, so much so that at one point we had adopted the *Bananas in Pyjamas* catch-phrase, "Are you thinking what I'm thinking, B1?"

Now, he shook his head and said, "Bro, you know I have a family to take care of now! How do you expect me to be a family man and carry your ass as well?"

I stared in silence, my bloodshot eyes accusing him of being inconsiderate. He continued, determined to see his speech through to the end.

"And your mother needs you right now. How do you think this is affecting her? You need help. You need to get over your fucking loneliness issues."

I was hurt; and extremely offended. Who the hell did he think he was? What gave him the right? What gave him the right to preach to me about issues of any sort? He didn't… He couldn't understand what I felt. At least his father had been around to give him a normal family. His father *wanted* him. He had pictures and all the perks I was denied. He couldn't know how it felt to be rejected by someone you never even met or what it was like to idolise your best friend who taught you nearly everything and have him tell you he couldn't be that man anymore. I got up in silence and went to the door.

Without turning around, I pulled it open and said, "Patrick, fuck off."

It would be close to four years before we ever spoke again.

Mother didn't get any better. Most nights she was delirious. She would shout at students who were now grown men with families. But on the eve of my thirtieth birthday she was calm. She seemed more like herself than she had in a long time. She asked if I had reconnected with my imaginary friends yet. We both chuckled. I told her she could pick any book she wanted and I would start reading right there with her. She laughed – a frail sound that barely escaped her lips – and said she wasn't quite ready to join me in the land of one book too many. We both laughed again. She looked at me and smiled. Even then her smile was utterly beautiful. It broke my heart. It took some time for me to see that she was gone. Her breathing had stilled, and when I shook her there was no response. My world crumbled.

I wept all night. I had lost the rock that had been there all my life. I had never even considered the reality of a world without her.

I wept all night.

When the preparations for the funeral began the following day, I disappeared inside a bottle of gin. By the time the funeral came I had drunk myself beyond oblivion. I wish I could tell you how beautiful the service was; or how peaceful she looked in her coffin. But I couldn't bear the pain of saying goodbye so I wasn't there to witness any of that. I lost count of the bottles I downed each day to dull the ache. Losing Patrick was one thing. When all was said and done, he was just a friend. Now I had lost the one person who had never once judged me; the one person who considered me wonderful even when I was spiralling towards skid row.

I remember, though, that I was at Centenary Park after we buried her. Her fountain had become mine. People walked past me and burned holes in my flesh with their judgement. I could not have cared less. The gin had managed, at least for the time being, to reduce the searing pain in my breast to a distant throb. I nearly dropped my bottle at the sound of mother calling my name. I looked up and there she sat on the edge of the fountain. She looked twenty-five years younger, her hair was the jet black it had been in my childhood. Tears streaked down her face as she looked at me, and my heart broke all over again. Barely coherent I asked her why she was grieving.

"You know why," she said. "Can you really not see what a mess you are? I can't believe this is how you want the world to remember the son I raised!"

I could say nothing. Bitter tears burned my cheeks. She told me it would be OK if I just let go of the bottle. She told me she missed me. That she missed coming to the fountain to talk like in the old days. I had heard all this while she was ill. Hearing the same words from this renewed apparition stung even more. I got up and tried to hug her, but she was gone. Instead I fell headlong into the fountain.

When I came to, I lay in a pool of my own vomit on the pavement a few metres from the fountain. I had no sense of what day it was, and my head screamed Ave Maria. Bitch of a hangover. But something was different.

I didn't want to drink anymore.

Stanza 7: Quitters Live Longer

It would be the easiest thing in the world to gloss things over and say that was the end of it; that from that day on not a single drop of alcohol passed my lips and I lived happily ever after. But that would be a shamefaced lie.

It was a struggle.

For months my mother's youthful ghost haunted me and assured me that I could let go. Each visit was more encouraging than the last. I would be sober for weeks and then slip and slide, first rationalising that I was doing well and convincing myself that one beer would be a good reward for my effort. Of course, the problem with people like me is that one beer will never be one beer. The night of reward would spiral into the morning of regret. Then one afternoon I was idly reading the Jobs Wanted ads at Haddon 'n' Sly when an Alcoholics Anonymous poster caught my eye. The man on it looked normal. No signs of the inebriation that I knew he, like me, would find at the bottom of the Gordon's Gin he was holding by its neck, just the same way I was holding my Gilbert's. His image stayed with me, materialising every time I went into the supermarket, each time I came across the piece of paper where I'd written down the number. That paper spent a year tucked into the corner of a frame that held my mother's picture. Eventually I found the courage to call.

Our meetings were held at the Helicopter of Christ Church. The booming voice on the phone had given me directions to 'our church' without being specific and when I finally got to the repurposed factory at the corner of Fifteenth and Fort Street, I stood staring at the banner for a few minutes. It looked like the kind of thing that had been made by the self-proclaimed graphic designers who appeared all over town as computers became more affordable. It was altogether too busy. The purple and white background was almost obscured by a picture of the Pastor (and most likely the church's founder) and a woman I assumed to be his wife. Next to them Word Art was used to produce the words "Helicopter of Christ Church" in a golden cursive font. Beneath the pair, the mandatory catch phrase promised 'Healing and Deliverance through Our Lord Jesus Christ.' Below that the service days and times were squeezed in along with a footnote that the pastor could be seen in his office at all other times.

The booming voice belonged to Pastor Ikechukwu Esomnofu. He waited just inside the building introducing himself and welcoming people to the meeting. He had gained weight since the photo on the banner and he spoke in a staccato that I had come to associate with Nollywood Movies. He was quick to tell me that I could call him Pastor Ike, adding – with a short laugh – that Pastor Esomnofu was his father. His wife, Ngozi, served cooldrink and biscuits for the meeting then faded into the background as the ritual storytelling began.

Pastor Ike welcomed us all to get things warmed up. He told us how the devil had once trapped him in the bottle. I rolled my eyes, but I didn't leave. By then I was well and truly convinced that I could not stop drinking on my own. I listened to a few speakers with increasing hope that the itch could be overcome. There were men who told stories of how they lost wives, children, siblings, jobs, and their dignity. One old man with a voice full of gravel and one good eye said he had found himself living in the streets with only the clothes on his back and a photo of his daughter. He didn't know where she was now. He'd returned to his former house to find that it had been sold while he roamed the streets. None of the neighbours could tell him what had become of his daughter.

It would be a few weeks before I gathered the courage to tell my own story. I never really subscribed to the idea of a sponsor. I was afraid I would become too dependent, but on my rough days Pastor Ike and the one-eyed man were available at the church. I would go and argue with them about God and religion until I was sure the urge had passed.

Eventually, I got clean.

One of the harder things to believe when I first started the journey back from my self-styled Valhalla was how empty my grandfather's house was. I had pawned most of the furniture. At the time it seemed like a good idea. A fat bank account can only last so long when you're unemployed and drinking like you own the brewery. But it didn't worry me. I felt like superman. I was kicking the habit. Life could not get any better. I was the man.

But I needed a job. I wrote what I believed to be a glowing cover letter and woke up each day dropping applications at every company I thought might need extra hands. Finding a job was harder than losing one. Things had changed so much in the preceding years. Most companies were firing instead of hiring. So I took up reading again. Words were my greatest companions during my formative years and I was sure that our reunion would be a joyous one. I joined the only library I knew, the one on Fort and Eighth. I had embarrassed myself too many drunken times to have any reservations about rubbing shoulders with high school kids. In between my long walks from First Avenue to Donnington – dropping CVs and enquiring within where there were signs inviting jobseekers to do so – I immersed myself in the nostalgic scent of books bought long before I was born. Re-establishing my pace was easy. The gentleman at the check-out desk was often surprised at how quickly I returned books.

I was unemployed for months and I read like a maniac. On some days I would choose a small book and read the whole thing in the library before picking something much larger to take home. I'd developed a keen interest in the history of the Nguni and Peter Becker's *Path of Blood* was at the top of my reading list. I had read his other book on my hero, Shaka, and was curious to know what he had to say about uMzilawegazi, the great scion of Ndaba, and his Matabele warriors. *Path of Blood* was in the library catalogue, but each search was less hopeful than the last.

On one particular day, I was wondering if someone had added it to their personal collection when I noticed a pretty woman sitting in one of the chairs at the end of the section. She was deeply engrossed in some enormous encyclopaedia. I was gob smacked. I rarely met other adults at the library, probably because they were at work, and this one was simply captivating. Skinny jeans were the in thing at the time and hers hugged her legs so tight I hoped they would rip open. Her black t-shirt bore the legend: "You call me bitch like it's a bad thing' and her modest chest rose and fell slowly with each breath she took. Her face was concealed under a large khaki sunhat. I've told a lot of lies in my lifetime and to say that I was not attracted by her body – and the legend on her shirt – would be a poor attempt at adding to the list. I stood staring, unable to think of a single thing to say. All thoughts of Becker and Mzilikazi relegated to the furthest wastelands of my mind.

Without looking up from her book she said, "You might as well take a picture."

It hadn't occurred to me that she could see me, or that she was paying attention to me.

"Forgive me," I croaked, "But it's not every day that one stumbles, quite literally, on such beauty."

"And what would 'one' know about beauty?" Eyes still glued to her encyclopaedia.

I couldn't help grinning. It had been years since I read *The Prophet*, and I seized the opportunity to quote from it.

"Not much," I began.

"Beauty is when life unveils her holy face.

But you are life and you are the veil.

Beauty is eternity gazing at itself in a mirror.

But you are eternity, and you are the mirror."

She said nothing, and for a moment continued to stare at her book. Then she looked up at me with an incredulous grin. Even in the dim light of the library I could see her striking brown eyes. They were full of life and confidence. A man could get lost in those eyes.

And I dove in.

Stanza 8: Beloved

Thandiwe brought a presence in my life that I had never experienced. I have been with many women, mostly prostitutes in need of a constant john minus the nagging about their smoking and partying, but none of them ever possessed me the way she did. She was beautiful, and my senses collapsed under the weight of my desire for her.

We talked non-stop from the day we met. If I wasn't delivering CVs I was sitting among the piles of t-shirts in her rented room in Magwegwe North, talking about everything and nothing. The t-shirts were how she made a living. She printed them for churches, corporates and the occasional wedding or birthday party. Those were the only ones with repetitive designs; the rest bore whimsy like "Here comes trouble" and "Buck Fob."

"It isn't Gucci," she said when she first let me into her room, "but at least it pays the rent and keeps me out of trouble."

We would chat while she worked, and when I got home we'd send each other SMSs all night. The stories were infinite; secrets flew across the airwaves, back and forth. I told her things about myself that even Patrick didn't know. All my darkest fears and obsessions were laid bare. It was liberating to give myself so completely to someone and have them do the same. I told her how low I had sunk during the worst of my drinking. She laughed. She had just finished a batch of one hundred t-shirts for Prophet Chindedza's annual "No More Shit" campaign. *The Sound of Silence* was playing from an mp3 disc that contained every genre imaginable, including urban grooves.

"You? An alcoholic? A trashcan alcoholic?" she laughed and shook her head in disbelief. "You look more like a panty sniffer if you ask me."

"A panty sniffer?"

"Yes. You know... those guys who sneak into women's rooms and sniff their underwear? Your big all-over-the-place eyes fit the profile perfectly."

We both laughed. Her teasing was something I would grow to

love as the weeks and months rolled by. She became a prominent part of my thoughts even before I realised that I was falling for her. All the worst parts of my life faded away to nothing when I was with her. I had spent so long trying to find this feeling at the bottom of a bottle. I was happy at last, and I found myself warming up to the idea of marriage and kids.

I was smitten.

Eventually, I found someone willing to employ me. The old lady didn't care that I was a recovering drunk. She needed an Office Assistant, which was a polite way of saying she wanted an errand boy. The money was good enough though, so I didn't mind. I spent most of my days reading at my desk. The time I spent fetching dry-cleaning or typing pages out of her religious guide felt more like taking a break than working. It was a start and what's more it presented the opportunity to take things further with Thandiwe.

We moved in together even before my first pay came. We had long since outgrown the short commute between our houses. Texting all night felt like trying to drink the ocean with a teaspoon. I wanted her close to me all the time. I was prepared to go the distance with her. Her things blended in quite well with my nothing.

Soon enough my grandfather's house began to resemble a home once more.

Stanza 9: Et Tu, Brute?

Two weeks ago, I had the worst headache I can remember having outside of a hangover. It was one of those Fridays when my employer tried to keep me busy by asking me to type out some pages from her religious guide. After battling with ten pages or so I decided that there was no shame in going home early. I needed to nurse my headache for the rest of the day. Thandiwe, as always, would be busy with her work, but I knew she would take a break to make sure I was alright.

I got out and dragged myself to TM Hyper. I dozed in the front seat of the kombi while we waited for other passengers, silently thanking God that the car radio was missing. It was a few minutes to lunchtime and already some of the younger schoolchildren could be seen going this way and that. Some were already catching lifts to their respective homes while others decided to take advantage of the afternoon. The boys would probably spend it playing video games at Bison's on Ninth Avenue. I couldn't even attempt a guess at how the girls would spend theirs.

By the time I dropped off at my stop my head was pounding. Faces I had been seeing my whole life swam past as I ambled towards my home, thinking I might never wake up from the nap I would take that afternoon. The front door was locked. Nothing odd there, perhaps she had gone to the shops. Focusing on one movement at a time, I fished the keys out of my pocket, selected the right one and unlocked the door. There was a rushing in my ears like a distant waterfall. I was desperate to lie down and close my eyes.

I open the door and am confronted by the convulsing buttocks of an elderly man. I can tell he is elderly because his buttocks are wrinkled. It strikes me that this is one rarely-mentioned sign of ageing. Perhaps I consider this for a moment too long, perhaps because I can only stand there and watch, dumbstruck. They are unaware of me, the two illicit lovers, and they continue with their foul act. The old geezer writhes and groans, I can even hear gurgling sounds as if he is drooling onto my Thandiwe. She squeals beneath him, her moans high-pitched and breathy. When she opens her eyes she falls silent for a moment and then pushes at the man who is still thrusting into her, his face now buried in her neck. She is shouting my name, trying to buck him off her.

"There is no Victor here," he gasps, still thrusting, "only this raging Buffalo."

He sounds like he is exerting himself, breathless. I can see him exerting himself and it's as if I'm mesmerised by his movements. His buttocks clench and unclench. I hate myself for the fog in my brain, for the hammer hidden beneath the fog. Something is happening, and I should be moving, doing something, saying something; but I say and do nothing.

I know that voice very well. I heard it often when I was growing up. It could be heard every night shouting from beyond the fence in the house that was within touching distance of ours. The owner of that voice is the reason why Mrs Nyathi preferred to come over to this house to watch me back when I needed babysitting, instead of me being taken to hers as was usual with other babysitters in the area. I have not had much contact with the Nyathis for many years. Usually because I was too drunk to make conversation, and lately because I was too occupied with Thandiwe to bother with being neighbourly. And today, Mr Nyathi, my neighbour – formerly my grandparent's neighbour, whose wife was my babysitter – is on my Thandiwe. Fucking the happiness I waited for, for so long, out of my life.

The pain, so sudden and so undeserved, sends me into red rage. As I step forward the old man seems to realise that Thandiwe is trying to show him something. His head is met by a young cuckold's fist as he turns to see what it is. It sounds like a dull slap against a wall. A faint whimper escapes his lips. I've never used my fists until today; I am surprised by how easily it comes. I land a second, third, fourth and fifth punch. I lose all control. Somewhere far off, I can hear my own enraged voice. Roaring "you motherfucker!" repeatedly above the sound of Thandiwe pleading with me to

Stop it, Victor, pleeeeeaase!

She tries to pull me away from the old man. Later I will wonder how hard I really pushed her. Right now, she collapses against the wall and looks at me with fear in her eyes. For a moment, that look gives me a strange sense of satisfaction. But I am not done with the old Buffalo just yet.

Sometime later, I am lifted off Nyathi in a full nelson hold. He is unconscious, but still I struggle to get free and finish what I started. A bigger man holds me tight, too tight for me to free myself. He is my other neighbour. Somehow Thandiwe got dressed up and went for help. The man does not let me go until the police arrive. Rightfully so, because all I have on my mind is murder. I don't know how much time has passed since I opened that door. Nyathi is taken away in an ambulance and the police escort me to 'the stocks.'

Nyathi was in such bad shape he spent the week in hospital. I spent the same week locked up alone with my thoughts. The cell was dark, even during the day. I watched other prisoners come and go, stuck in my cell until Nyathi died or was discharged. One man, a skinny fellow whose much-broken nose revealed his eagerness to emphasise his point with fists, decided the toilet and the only available blanket were his, promising to make a wife out of anyone who tried to use either. We all understood what he meant, and I was willing to shit right in my pants rather than be sodomised. Like everyone else I made do with the other corner of the cell. The filth could not have gotten any worse. Another cellmate had a cough so bad I was convinced his brief visit had left us all with a generous helping of TB. One by one they came and went while I waited for someone to come for me. Even Thandiwe.

She didn't come. Why would she? What would we say to each other? I barely slept. In my loneliness and hunger my mind began to mutiny. So I prayed. After a life of making fun of Christians about praying to Senior, Junior and the Spook I prayed like hell. I prayed forgiveness for the drinking, for the whores of my past and for every impure thought I ever had. I pleaded with God to let me out. I swore I would change. I promised I would never harm another human being again if he just let me out of there.

Evidently, that promise was a lie.

Stanza 10: The Clearing at the End of the Path

The charges were dropped. Old Mr Neighbourly was more concerned with keeping his name out of the papers. Upon my release I went straight to the house to find it deserted. She had taken her things and left. She hadn't even bothered to lock the door. I flopped onto my bed and screamed. Then I slept like I had never slept before.

I spent a few days lying in bed, staring at the ceiling and wondering what to do next. I was alone, and my heart still bled profusely. Thandiwe had brought joy to my life and in an instant Nyathi fucked it all up. And now she was gone. I was alone. I wanted to die.

If whoring can be compared to art, then Nyathi was Michelangelo. Even when I was a child it was a well-known fact that he spent a lot of his time trying to fuck anything in a skirt and his success rate was legendary. That fact alone made going to the New Start Centre a terrifying idea.

When I finally got to the testing centre, I sat through the pre-test counselling wondering if Thandiwe had gone back to her old room. Had she ever been tested? I could check on my way back home. Presently I sat in a group with several other people who had come to check their status. A young man to my left looked like God had found him pissing in the altar wine. The bored old counsellor peered over her glasses at all of us as she gave us the old speech.

"Please stay until your results come. Whatever happens here today, you must know that HIV is not a death sentence. Many people have lived with the virus for years and now it can be treated."

When the counselling session ended, we all went in for the test; one by one. After the test I knew what the result was the minute that woman started talking. I am HIV positive. But I am not going to spend the rest of my life dancing to the tune of some little virus. Thandiwe made sure of that. The world at last, had found a way to clean up its mess. I was, after all, a mistake. The unexpected spawn of two teenage lovers, one of whom had a deep desire to show her mate how much she adored him, and the other with a deep desire to satisfy a bulging erection.

I wondered why I had never seen it before. I grew up surrounded by misery and loneliness. Of course the world had been pushing me towards elimination from the very day I was born! I was forced into this world out of the cosmos to a life of constant disappointment. I never had a chance. Finally, the world was being blunt: 'Close the door on your way out, please and thank you.' This time there was no denying it. The counsellor assured me that the rest of my life would still go on as normal. I left her with my assurance that she was absolutely right.

As I walked out onto Eighth Avenue I thought about Thandiwe. I thought about those brown eyes with the slightest hint of hazel around the edges; about her long dreadlocks – she loved those dreadlocks – and her tiny, teardrop-shaped body. I thought about all the laughter-filled conversations we had over the past two years. I thought about how she had told me she never loved anyone the way she loved me. I thought about how much, even then, I still wanted her close to me. How much I still wanted to wrap my arms around her and smell her sweet perfume as our bodies reassured each other that everything would be fine; that we were finally home. Finally happy. But Nyathi's wrinkled form was superimposed over every memory I had. A familiar itch took over my throat. Donald Gilbert was calling my name again.

On my way home I bought a bottle of gin and a few cans of tonic at TM Hyper. Back at the house I opened the bottle and stared at it for a long time. Mother appeared again. She sat on the other side of the room, her eyes pleading with me not to take a sip. I closed my eyes and opened them again. She was still there, still pleading. So I closed the bottle and lay on the bed, thinking about Thandiwe.

But that was last week. This week I spent a lot of time thinking about birth. When I was born, I wept and the world rejoiced. I wonder if anyone will weep as I am born again in a new world. Perhaps one in which joy is all I will ever know. I hadn't had a drink until today. Of that, at least, I can be proud. But now that my tale is told I have allowed myself a final kiss with the bottle. Mother hasn't left. Her eyes are not pleading anymore. She stares now with what I think is sadness… and disappointment.

Did I tell you about the revolver on my desk? I was surprised by the ease with which one can get one's hands on a gun in Bulawayo. But that is a story for another writer. In just moments, I will have completed the job that nature has repeatedly failed to do. If the drugged liquor fails then the revolver will send me to the clearing at the end of the path.

Today is a special occasion. My thirty-third birthday will see me take the path taken by many of the greats. Maybe on the other side I'll be able to have a drink or two with Hemmingway and Ingrid Jonker; Shakespeare too if the rumours are to be trusted. I hope I won't have to use the gun. I called Patrick a few minutes ago. We wouldn't want him to get here while I'm still thrashing about in the throes of death.

THE HUNT

After sixteen years of my father's rigorous training, he took me up into the mountain and performed the rites of initiation himself. It was a proud, long awaited, moment. On my first day as a man I recited the lessons of the fathers. Father listened – smiling a little. On our way down, Father said we would go on the next hunt together.

Hunting had always been Father's job. He would disappear sometimes, only to return a month or more later, carrying sun dried cow, goat, eland, and – one time – zebra meat. He hunted with the knobkerrie and one of a variety of spears from his handcrafted collection of homemade weapons. Someday his weapons would be my weapons. He was the only one who could see the outside world. I had longed to see what lay beyond the eucalyptus trees since I was a little boy.

When we left a few weeks later, my mother and sisters were up early with us, praying for a bountiful journey. Mother kissed me on the forehead. Her farewell was a reluctant one. She still called me Bhabha, a word I said ceaselessly as a toddler according to her, even though I had earned my father's name through the initiation. I had never spent time away from her, but my eagerness to see the outside far outweighed my anxiety. The two little girls hugged me simultaneously. Then we left. The homestead lay hidden inside a valley, and we made it to its boundary in time to watch the sun rise at home for the last time. And then we were past the eucalyptus trees and walking, hidden in the grass. It was safer to go north. Most things that went south never came back. The few things that did were never the same. South Africa had been heavily involved in the war, and generations later the air was still foul with its residue. Which isn't to say there were no mutants in the north, it was just less likely that your paths would cross.

We mostly walked through the bush. What little was left of the roads the old people built was also overrun by wild plants, and you were more likely to get lost if you followed them. Father knew the route well. We took a few detours so he could show me some relics of the time before the war. The first detour was my favourite. We wandered into an abandoned home around midday on our first day. Just inside the gate was a rusted old triangular thing with three tooth rimmed circles on one corner, and a forked piece of metal on the other. Father eyed it curiously, poking at the teeth with the tip of his knobkerrie.

"I wonder what this was," he muttered.

"A weapon, perhaps?" I offered.

He tried to push it with his knobkerrie, grunting slightly. Then he shook his head. "I tried picking it up the first time I saw it. You would get tired of carrying it very fast."

"Unless you were very strong..."

That made him laugh, "Unless you were very strong."

He warned against going inside the houses as we left the contraption and went on our way, "You don't want to frighten a hiding mutant into fighting you."

I shuddered at the image of a mutant sinking its teeth into my flesh in defence of its territory. They were known to bite if backed into a corner. And some simply because they could. The home was also the first of many markings on the route Father wanted me to learn well for future hunting trips.

We saw a mutant a day before we reached Inyathi. The creature nibbled at the leaves of a dry acacia tree. A third eye stared blindly at us from its rump, and I could not remove mine from the malformed fifth leg that hung revoltingly where its left ear should have been. Blood poured from a wound on its flank, and even from where we watched its stench was thick.

"This must be descended from goats," Father whispered. We made a detour around the goat-thing and kept walking. Mutant meat is toxic. Anyone foolish enough to eat it dooms himself to a painful, burning death. The disease it caused progressed quickly from a slight headache to painful, exploding blisters oozing blood that had begun to congeal in your veins. Father had watched his last friend kill and eat a mutant when the hunting trips had begun to lengthen. He had never forgotten it. And he made sure I knew.

Inyathi was my great grandfather's birthplace. Its buildings stood in ruin. Father blamed it on poor design along with nature. Trees and grass grew inside the buildings, almost as if nature had vowed to reclaim the land civilization had taken from her. At the front of the building there was a large sign. Father said the old people had used public storehouses like this to keep their supplies. Currently it was just an empty shell. We walked on until dusk and laid camp by a stream beyond Inyathi.

After we had finished the day's rations, Father sat down on the other side of the fire and looked at me.

"Son," he said, then fell silent.

"Baba," I addressed him formally as he had done with me.

"Putting aside the mutated goat we saw yesterday," he began, shifting his eyes to the dying fire between us, "how many animals have you seen since we left home?"

I shook my head slowly, thinking back over the preceding days.

"That's right," he said, calmly massaging the knuckles of his right hand with his left, "just that mutie fucking goat."

He sat in silence for a while. I stared fixedly at the fire.

"Son," he said again, "why do we hunt?"

"Because we need meat."

"And why do we need meat?"

"Meat is the only food that won't kill you, provided it doesn't come from a mutant."

"Provided it doesn't come from a mutant," he repeated.

He raised his eyes to mine briefly, then said, "Mutants are all there is. I haven't seen a non-mutant animal since before your grandfather died. Do you remember him?"

Grandfather died when I was a little boy. Before my little sisters were born. I vaguely remembered him as a scratchy drawl and the faint smell of smoke. He told stories about how the rabbit gave the lion his roar. Something had been wrong with Grandfather's chest at the end. Something to do with the grass he gathered, dried and smoked. Now I nodded in disbelief and pointed to the discarded leaf that had carried the day's rations; opening my mouth to ask the question, dreading the answer.

"Mutants? Have you been catching mutants??" I gasped.

He shook his head immediately, "Mutant meat is toxic. You know that."

He stared into the dying embers of the fire for a while. I could tell he was struggling to find the words.

"I have gone deeper and deeper inland during the last few years," he reached over to his left to pick up a small stick and began to poke the embers. "There is one thing that is still thriving even now, with all the mutants and the filth in the air…"

I looked at my father, horrified. My mind ran back to all the times he had come back from hunting. Each time he stated that he had caught a different animal. A wild cow lost in the bush; a small eland; once he had even said the only thing he could find was a lone Zebra. But the thing I kept going back to wasn't the names of the animals he brought home. It was the way the meat tasted. So sweet, so tender and delicious after mother broiled it relentlessly.

But it all tasted the same. I had never questioned it until now. Now that Father was sitting across from me, telling me that he had not seen a single animal in all that time. I felt dizzy and sick. I opened my mouth to accuse Father but instead all the meat we had just consumed came rushing out and onto the orange glow of what remained of the fire, effectively putting it out.

I stood up, unable to make sense of it all. Still I worked up the courage to ask.

"If not mutants," I choked, "then what?"

My father looked at me morosely, "I can see by your reaction that you have figured it out."

"Monster," I roared, "Monster!"

"It's the only food out there that won't kill you, Son. You said it yourself."

I picked up the spear at my side.

"They were brothers and sisters…" I spat. "They were fathers!

Sons!"

"They were the only food we could eat and not burn to death!" he retorted.

I leapt over the fire, spear in hand, and rage in my gut. I wanted to drive it into his heart. I didn't see him pick up the knobkerrie; I only became aware of it when he used the shaft to deflect my spear. I fell awkwardly to his left and, before I could react, he put his arms around me and whispered in my ear for me to calm down. That he would let me go if I would just calm down. Hot tears stung my eyes and then ran down my face. All the while I struggled against my father's embrace. He was still twice my size, but I wriggled and kicked hard enough for us to fall over. Eventually my strength began to wane and all I could do was weep in my father's arms. I retched painfully a couple of times but nothing more came out. When he felt me begin to relax, he cautiously let me go.

Without warning, three men materialised out of the darkness. Each carried large branches that had been crudely carved into a shape not dissimilar to the one father had often shown me before. A club he said he used to brain his prey. Like us, these men wore clothes from before. Clothes that the old people made in reckless abundance, as if they believed they would live forever, according to Mother. It was too dark to make out much of their features, but one thing was certain, these men were not here to make friends.

Father was on his feet immediately.

"Madoda," he said, "we are hunters. In search of food for our family. I can see…"

"Shut your mouth old man," one of them hissed, "story time is over."

"We've been looking for you, mdala," said another. This one repeatedly tapped his left palm with the large end of his club.

The first man spoke again, "We'd begun to think you wouldn't come back. Almost hoped it was over. But here you are."

"Here I am," I heard father say through clenched teeth.

I wanted to ask who these men were, why they would be looking for father, but fear wired my jaw shut. They had formed a triangle around us, and just beyond the feet of the one who had spoken first I could see the shape of Father's leather sack. Our weapons! Dismay washed over me like the darkness around us.

The third man finally spoke up, "Did you enjoy my brother? Did he feed you well?"

I felt my heart sink even lower. Revenge. These men were here to avenge the people father had killed. The people we had consumed. The people we had come here to hunt. I looked at Father. He said nothing. The man who had just spoken poked at Father's chest with the fat end of his club.

"Did you think we wouldn't find you?" he asked.

Father said nothing. This seemed to infuriate the man because he raised his club high, intending to bring it down on his head. It never found its mark. Father lunged forward and tackled him. As they fell Father's voice filled the night.

"BALEKA!"

He surprised all of us. The other two turned their attention to this unexpected turn of events and rushed forward to help their comrade. I didn't need to be told that word twice. I sprang up and bolted into the darkness. Into lands unknown. Small branches slapped my face and scratched my legs as I ran, sure I could hear one of the men thundering after me in their own territory. I did not know where I was going. Only that I had to run as far and as fast as I could away from these men whose relatives we had eaten.

I ran.

And as I began to tire the ground disappeared from under me. I flew downwards briefly before I came crashing down on my bum. Lightning shot up my lower back and I howled as I slid forward and downwards. I flailed wildly, wanting to grab onto something. Anything. But all I got was air. Then my feet struck something solid. There was a loud crack and my world became pain. I had stopped, but my legs hurt in ways I had never known they could hurt. I screamed into the night. I screamed for what seemed an eternity. Then I lay there sobbing.

I haven't moved since then. Any movement seems to multiply

the pain several times. So I've just been lying here. Listening to the breeze whisper through the trees. Watching the sky turn from last night's dark pattern of stars to today's blue and closing my eyes against the ferocious heat of the sun.

It's starting to get dark again.

Tonight, surely, Father will come for me.

He must come for me.

The pain in my legs is unbearable.

My back…

…Oooh my back.

I wish Mother was here.

SIRENS

Mlungisi, engulfed by an overwhelming sense of urgency in life, walked into Gramps' Tavern and sat down at his favourite spot at the bar. More than ever, he felt that the possibility of death had ceased to be something in the distant future and had rather become a tangible part of his existence. He watched the barmaid as she poured relief into a tall glass. He loosened his tie and pulled it over his head. Her beauty was always one of the things he loved most about the tavern. He told as many people as he possibly could about her smooth golden skin, her petite waist juxtaposed with her modest hips and bottom, and especially about her legs that went on forever. In these stories he called her The Thoroughbred.

They made small talk as she worked. He had become something of a regular at the tavern. The booze was reasonably priced, the food was decent, and he rarely met anyone there whose vocabulary included the words 'swag' or 'blesser.' The Thoroughbred seemed to consider him a friend. She knew without being told when he was there for the good old sundowner. She knew when some old wounds needed dabbing with alcohol. If the place wasn't busy, she would chat him up relentlessly. Mlungisi didn't mind. Gramps' Tavern was the only place in Harare where his disdain for the city dissolved into a sense of familiarity and warmth. The younger woman's attention and her sultry voice were a welcome addition. He would often indulge her tales that ranged from abusive neighbours and their shenanigans to distant relatives whose lover's infidelity had given them an excuse to ferry themselves across the Styx.

"Don't forget to put that in your jacket," she said and gestured toward his tie on the counter. Her Ndebele was fluent, with only the ghost of a Shona accent creeping around the edges of her speech; rearing its head in the overly explosive sound when she said 'jacket.'

"I wouldn't dare," Mlungisi jammed the tie into his pocket. It was company issued and his employer could fine him fifty dollars for losing it.

She smiled and went away to serve another customer. He drank from his glass, his eyes scanning the bar. The tavern was ancient; a relic of times when he would not have been allowed through the door. The wooden panelling was old but well taken care of. He spent most of his visits splitting his attention between the TV mounted above the bar and the mirror behind the various bottles of alcohol. Being able to see what was happening in the tavern through the mirror gave him an odd sense of comfort. Presently he chuckled, as he had done a few times before, at the various items that hung over the bar: a porcelain model of a Cocker Spaniel's head, a variety of mugs and vases, a couple of BSAP Caps, something that resembled a wooden club, a handwritten 'No Smoking' sign, and – his favourite – a plaque that bore a drawing of an old man with his nose buried in a book whose title read 'Old bookkeepers never die, they just lose their balance!'

Mlungisi's eyes drifted back to the mirror. The only other patrons were an old man who had been shouting on the phone since Mlungisi arrived and four young men immediately behind him who were talking about movies and surfing the internet. Music he should have been too young to enjoy filled the bar. It was Thursday. Ladies' Night was one of the tavern's busier nights and he knew that as soon the DJ arrived the bar would drown in new music. Mercifully, it was the bar manager's playlist that would dominate until then.

"The manager should be the DJ," he told no one in particular.

He submerged himself in the sound as more people trickled into the bar. A few of the other regulars greeted him as they lined up on either side of him. On the TV, a very one-sided soccer match was unfolding and Mlungisi fixed his eyes on this, trying to drown out thoughts about how truly terrible his life was.

His sister never stopped telling him to leave. She had done so again that morning.

"Just walk away man! That place is killing you. You need a new start. Johannesburg has buckets of opportunities for educated young men like you."

He only chuckled, "What happened to Africa that made us think running away from home is the solution to our problems?"

"Well, it is if staying is making you miserable. That company has turned you into a complainer."

He had grinned, "It is miserable, Busi, but it's a great place for educated young men like me to learn. One day it will be a funny addition to my coming up stories."

He knew she wasn't convinced, but the call had ended without any more arguments from her. She knew how determined he was to stay and make a name for himself in Zimbabwe. They came from four generations of migration, and Mlungisi was convinced the only way he could ensure a different life for the next generation was to stay and fight. To build a legacy. He knew the country well. He had worked all around it for close to ten years and knew where to find anything he wanted. A new country would mean all those years had been for nothing. He would have to start from scratch. And that aside, his home was the land of opportunity. For all the things that were wrong there was an opportunity to be a pioneer. Who could run away from that?

The Thoroughbred's voice returned him to the present, "Looks like you've finally decided to commit suicide today."

She had brought him a second round. He raised his eyes quizzically and she laughed.

"Mafight was greeting you and you were dead to the world." She gestured toward the back office.

He grinned and waved at Mafight, the barman who took over when The Thoroughbred's shift ended.

"I guess I was daydreaming," he said, still grinning, "wishing I was born rich instead of handsome."

She walked away in laughter. He sipped his beer somewhat cheerfully.

A new voice had joined the din in the bar. The severity of its accent drew Mlungisi's attention to his left.

"Tirikunwa swiCastle wena!" its owner was saying.

The gentlemen she was talking to grinned and chuckled. She grinned along with them. Her clothes could have been tattoos for the way they clung to her body. In a different world, Mlungisi thought, she could have been a model. She was snacking on a packet of roasted peanuts and maize. He turned his eyes back to the TV but kept his ears on the conversation. Her Shona was thick with the sound of Bulawayo.

As if by magic, or perhaps Divine Will, she came to stand in the empty space next to him. He looked at her. She was watching the football match. He looked at the screen and greeted her, watching her out of the corner of his eye.

"Sal'bonani, sisi."

She snapped her head in his direction in surprise, and then broke into a short laugh that warmed his soul.

"Yebo, bhudi," she said, smiling, "How did you pick me out?"

"Well, my Shona is atrocious, but your accent is worse."

She laughed again, slightly turning to face him.

"Then I guess I will have to improve it."

"Or you could keep it," he retorted, "and let it bring you voices from back home."

This time they both laughed. He studied her face. Now that she was close, he had a clearer view of the scars on her face. She was a pretty girl. Her face told the story of a hard life but when she laughed Mlungisi felt like he could buy her a castle. Maybe even two. They both sighed. It was as if the whole bar had emptied and they were alone. He offered her a drink. She declined.

"If I get thirsty I'll drink yours."

From there the conversation blundered clumsily along, as is often the case between two people whose meeting is purely coincidental. Inevitably it steered itself towards the question of where they came from in Bulawayo. She was from Riverside. He was from Matsh'amhlophe. They had grown up literally one neighbourhood from each other and yet they only got to meet in Harare. That struck her as funny.

Mlungisi told her about his nomadic ancestors and his desire for a more stable future for progeny. She said was the last child in a family of four girls. Her parents were ancient, and people had always assumed she was her oldest sister's daughter. She laughed at that, her eyes brimming with nostalgia. A brief silence followed. She waved her hand as if to dispel the memories with a physical gesture.

"Anyway that was a lifetime ago. How is Bulawayo? I haven't been there in ages."

Mlungisi raised an eyebrow and asked, "How come? Don't you miss your family?"

"My sisters are all abroad and my parents are dead. What would I go back to? Empty rooms and fading memories? No thanks."

Mlungisi didn't know what to say next. He heard himself say he was very sorry for her loss. She simply shrugged.

The hours roll by quickly when people sit and talk in bars. Suddenly, the tavern was packed. A huge crowd milled around the stage where the DJ and a guest hostess were thrilling them with games that put men on display for the ladies. By then Mlungisi and his new friend were shouting to be heard.

"Are you sure you don't want that drink?" He asked, signalling Mafight to bring him another round.

She shook her head, "I told you we can share yours if the need arises!"

Mafight brought Mlungisi's drink. He took a sip and watched her, bobbing her head to the music vibrating in the walls. He wasn't a huge fan of Zim-dancehall, but it was catchy, and he found himself bobbing as well.

"You wanna dance?"

She led him away from the bar by his free hand before he could answer. Once they were on the dance floor, she took his beer and drank. They danced. One hand rested delicately on his right shoulder and the other clutched their beer, her eyes locked on his. When Mlungisi danced his reservations about the music on offer disappeared. She seemed to have relaxed as well. Each new song brought them closer together. A few songs later they were still going, close enough now that the scent of her lip gloss was deep inside his nostrils. He could all but taste her lips already. Her breath came in short gasps. Her movements had slowed. When she closed her eyes he leaned in closer still.

Her lips raped his senses. Electricity ran through his body. Later he would wonder if this was what people described as a toe-curling kiss. Their lips produced a faint smack as she pulled back. She struggled to conceal her smile. Her eyes searched his. He leaned in and kissed her again. She went limp for a second and then pressed her body against his. When she pulled back the smile was no longer concealed. She turned around and pushed her back into his chest as she resumed dancing. His hands dropped to her hips. Elliot Manyika's voice accompanied them. She bent over and began to draw sine waves in the air with her buttocks. She danced the kongonya like a pro and he followed, almost falling over her a few times.

It was something of a relief when she signalled that she needed to catch her breath. His neck glistened with sweat. He had been a desk jockey for ages and struggled to recall when last he had seen the inside of a gym. Still he ignored his hammering heart – and the clogged-up feeling in his ears – and followed her back to the bar. There was only one free stool and she took it. He leaned on the counter next to her. He motioned to Mafight for another round. When it came, she took it before he could and drank from the bottle. Then she handed it to him and let out an exaggerated sigh of refreshment. He smiled and drank.

Later they walked in the scant light of the buildings adjacent to the street. His arm had found its way around her waist and they staggered up Fourth Street. Their conversation continued in hushed tones. The neighbourhood had once been considered upmarket. His building was one of the many lonely old places in the area whose history could be told by looking around the grounds. The parking lot was a mess of potholes. Weeds had overrun the small children's playground and, during her only visit since he moved to Harare, his sister swore that you could get tetanus just by looking at the jungle gym. His current guest laughed in agreement.

The lights on the stairwell didn't work. Fortunately, they only had to go up one flight. She remarked how Western movies could be set in old buildings like these along with cities that had far outgrown pioneer imaginings. Here and more so back home, old buildings and decay were everywhere. They had arrived at his door. He held on to the doorframe and suggested that they discuss politics in the morning. On his third attempt he found the keyhole and she made a joke about his misses. He turned the key and assured her that there were some things he would never miss. He opened the door and led her in.

And now, my friends, I must avert my eyes. I am not one to spy on what happens between lovers behind closed doors. But Mlungisi awoke later to find that she was gone. All that remained was the lingering scent of her hair on the pillow next to his. That aside, it was like she hadn't even been there. He looked for her when he went to Gramps' Tavern. Repeatedly. Even years later, when he had several grey hairs on his head and the tell-tale beginnings of a lifelong stoop. He would sit at the tavern in an old black suit and a white shirt with the collar undone. The red tie would be in his pocket. A wry smile under his beard. His thoughts returned always to her hypnotic laugh and he wondered why he never thought to ask her name.

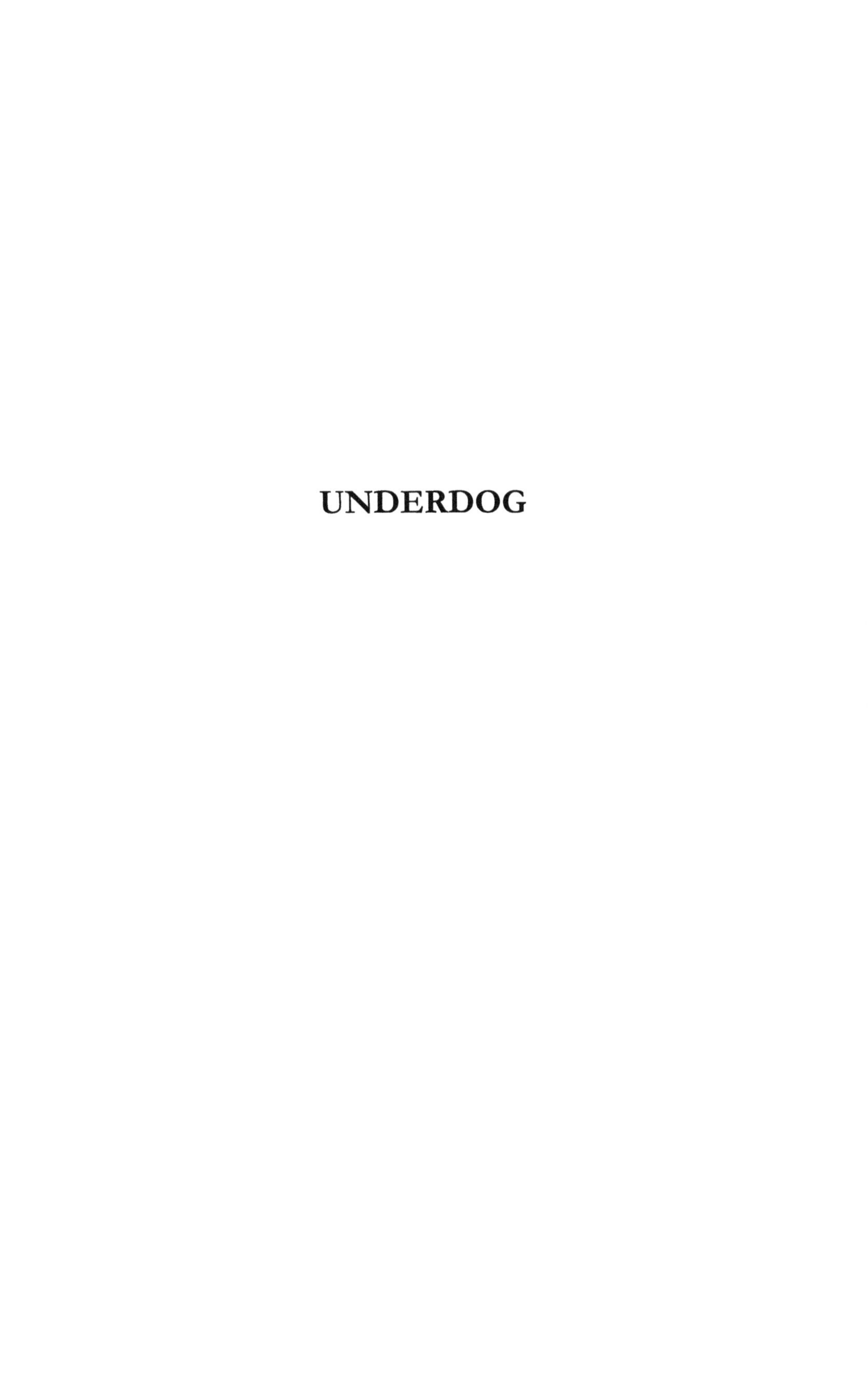

UNDERDOG

Mdluli sat in a camper chair with his rifle held firmly in his right hand. Next to him was a flask full of hot tea – rooibos or bust he always told his wife. He hated the winter. It brought longer nights and frosty mornings. In his present circumstances, it also brought longer guard shifts.

It was well past sunset. Night painted the sky black and all her minions had come out to terrorise anyone who dared to be outside their home. Cicadas and crickets flung their cryptic songs back and forth and, almost as if to remind him that he should not be out here, a bat flew drunkenly past Mdluli's face. He waved at it with his free hand and swore under his breath.

From where he sat, the view of his cattle pen was perfect. The stench of cow dung would have driven most people away. It got so far up your nostrils you could almost taste it, but Mdluli had lived on the farm his whole life. In time, everybody got used to the smell. Cattle-ranching was in his blood. His grandfather had worked as a black labourer on this same farm before Robert Mugabe took over. When the opportunity presented itself, his father snapped up the farm and Mdluli Farm was born.

Cattle were Mdluli's livelihood, and he would never sleep again if it meant he could protect them all.

ΔΔΔ

STOCK THEFT CASES ON THE RISE

May 4, 2020; Local News – The Chronicle

Mandla Dube, Matabeleland South Correspondent

Police in Matabeleland South have expressed concerns regarding the increase in cases of stock theft in the past few weeks.

"Matabeleland South has recorded over 30 missing cattle from various farms in the past 3 weeks alone," said Matabeleland South Provincial Police Spokesperson Inspector Nicholas Tshabangu.

He urged members of the public to ensure that their cattle were properly branded as the winter period set in to ensure that they can be identified. Inspector Tshabangu also emphasized the need for farmers to report the incidents as soon as they happen rather than waiting to report the case after losing two or more cattle.

"The problem we have is that some farmers only report the cases much later on when they see that the problem is continuing, and they have lost more cattle. We urge farmers to report immediately all stock theft, even if it is just one," Inspector Tshabangu said.

He also encouraged citizens to remain vigilant and to report any suspicious activities around their area.

– @Mindlos_Dubs

ΔΔΔ

Mdluli went to the police after the first bull disappeared. It was easy to believe that he had been targeted by cattle-thieves. His cattle ranked among the biggest and healthiest in the entire district. Every year he entered them for various prizes at the trade fair in Bulawayo and every year he won. Anyone who could sell his bull would have made more than just a pretty penny.

Nothing came of the police investigation. After spending more time at the station than he needed to, Mdluli decided to take matters into his own hands. He gathered all his herders and told them he would pay extra for anyone who stayed up and kept a watch every night until the culprits had been caught. He even hinted that if any of them should catch said culprits, then there would be a handsome reward for the man who did it.

For a few weeks there were no other disappearances. It was as if he had panicked for no reason. But just as he was starting to think he was wasting money on guard duty another bull disappeared. And soon after that a cow followed. Mdluli was furious. He fired the three boys and had them arrested. He had not worked so hard to have some ungrateful little boys steal his animals from right under his nose. What annoyed him most was the fact that he never retrieved his beasts. The police employed all their tactics of persuasion, but nothing came of it. The boys insisted they were not involved. When he couldn't take any more pain, one of the boys had claimed hideous beasts had shown up and devoured the cattle.

And then another bull disappeared. Mdluli was going out of his mind with frustration. And so he decided to mount a watch himself. He brought out an old AK47 he inherited from his father and sat by the cattle pen every night for a week.

He was entirely unprepared for what he saw on the eighth night.

ΔΔΔ

'FLYING DOGS ATE MY CATTLE' - GWANDA FARMER

May 26, 2020; Local News – The Chronicle

Mengezi Moyo, Matabeleland South Correspondent

A local man left police officers in stiches last week when he claimed that 'dogs with wings' were responsible for the recent increase in stock theft cases in the region.

Alex Nyathi (32), of Mdluli Farm on the Northern outskirts of Gwanda, tickled police officers at Gwanda Police Station last Thursday morning when he alleged that he had seen three creatures that resembled flying dogs attacking and devouring one of his cattle in the middle of the night. According to police officers who were present at the station, Nyathi claimed to have seen these dogs first 'sucking the life out of his bull, and then devouring the remains until nothing was left.'

Earlier this month, this paper carried a report on the increase in stock theft in Matabeleland South.

Mdluli, as Nyathi is popularly known in Gwanda, runs a cattle ranch in the area. According to neighbours, the Nyathi family has been raising cattle in the area since the early 2000s and since taking over from his late father in 2013, Mdluli has built a reputation as an intelligent, sober minded businessman.

"We were surprised to hear Mdluli coming with these strange claims," said one resident. "We know him to be a man of sober habits but I think that day he may have been drinking or smoking something."

Other residents suggested that the farmer was confused due to being attacked by the robbers.

Efforts to reach Nyathi for comment were fruitless.
- @MengeziMoyo

ΔΔΔ

Tonight, he was prepared. Thankfully, he thought, there had been no more disappearances in the few nights between. He suspected the dogs had gone to feed at other farms. Eventually they would return, and when they did, he would be ready with his trusted AK.

The creatures were not like anything he had seen before. They had massive wings that he supposed would compete with an eagle's in size. And they made no sounds except for the beating of their wings. It was as if they knew they had to be discreet. During that first encounter, Mdluli had been jerking in and out of sleep on his chair, wondering why he wasn't in his warm bed.

Initially he didn't take note of the sound of approaching birds. He had spent enough nights out in the open to know there were a lot of nocturnal creatures lurking, even on his property. But with every passing second the sound grew. The beating of wings became impossible to ignore. Mdluli raised his eyes and froze. Later that day, he would use the word 'dogs' to describe what he was looking at, but in truth they were not. The creatures he was looking at soared towards the cattle pen. The moonlight reflected off their dark hides. He found he still couldn't find the right words to describe the grotesque shapes that were supposed to be their heads. It was like something out of a low budget horror film from the 90s. But he never forgot the sharp teeth that kept their mouths open in a perpetual snarl. Nyathi wanted to scream, but his voice seemed to have gone on holiday.

The creatures swarmed around an unfortunate bull. There was no searching. No chasing the cattle around in the pen until they found the perfect one. It was as if they had followed a homing beacon to this specific one. They clung on to the beast using their talons and the mouths locked on to the poor bull's flesh. Mdluli watched as his beast thinned before his eyes. Later, he would think of it as drinking his bull. The bull stood in place and thinned until there was nothing left but hide and bone. But they did not stop there. They began to devour what remained. Mdluli finally found his voice. He screamed and then, for the first time in his life, he fainted. When he woke up the next morning he hoped he had dreamed it all, but he had a missing bull as expected.

Tonight, he was ready. Already he could hear the beating wings in the distance. He was prepared for a fight. He looked to the sky and saw three winged figures approaching his farm. His mind insisted on calling them dogs even now. He shuddered. The memory of what he had seen them do would never leave him. He quickly admonished himself for being a coward.

Everybody could laugh all they wanted.

"This is real," he muttered, bringing the butt of his AK47 to his shoulder.

He cocked the rifle and took aim.

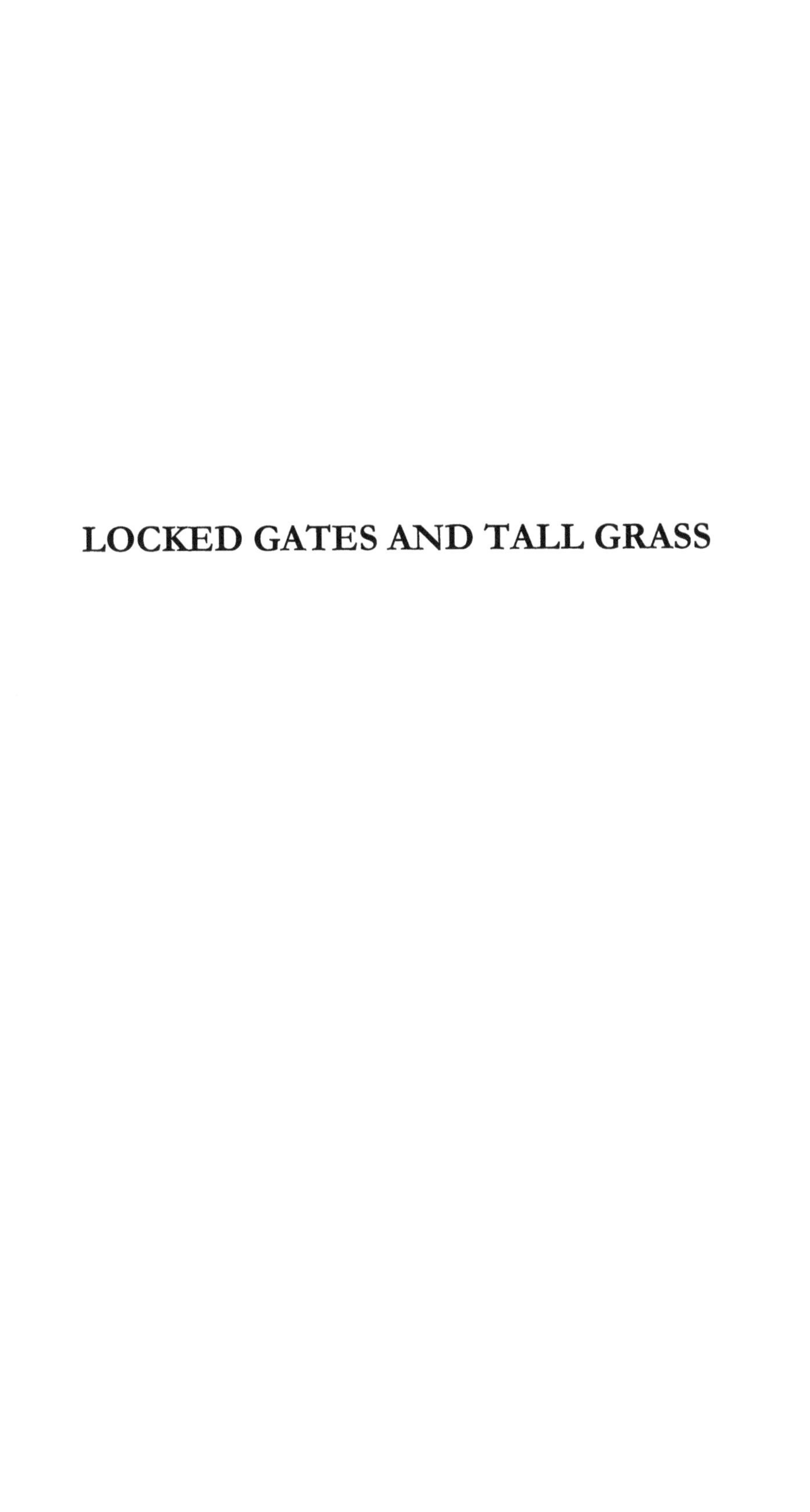

LOCKED GATES AND TALL GRASS

The lunchtime traffic swarmed around the brazen image of the nation's hero. Directly beneath him sat several photographers, each of whom found the area particularly good for business. Schoolteachers frequently brought their grade one classes on field trips to learn about 'Father Zimbabwe' and his selfless contribution towards gaining independence from the imperialists who wanted to enslave the black nation for eternity.

'Father Zimbabwe' stood on a pedestal right in the middle of the intersection of Eighth Avenue and the street named after him. Lungile stopped and stared at it for a few minutes. A roundabout had been constructed around it, giving people enough freedom to admire the statue without interfering with the traffic. The pedestal was at least three metres in height, and the effigy stood proudly on it with his short leadership staff in his right hand, forever gazing toward the north. Lungile chuckled. He was barely ten years old when the old man passed on, but he was certain that the statue looked nothing like him. He looked at the photographers all going about their business. To them the statue was a source of income, and it might as well have been Scooby Doo up there for all they cared. As always, they were busy attending to a group of schoolkids who wanted their picture taken. The kids loved the statue. In their eyes the old man was something of a legend. Lungile chuckled again. They would probably grow up knowing the only version of his story that the schools were permitted to teach.

The children gathered around the statue were from a school in Lobhengula West, where Lungile's family had lived many years ago. He would have recognised the uniform anywhere. Many of them were skinny and seemed malnourished. They wore ill-fitting uniforms that could easily have been bought when Lungile himself was in grade one.

So, this is the face of sovereignty, he thought.

His father, an incurable socialist – who, if Lungile's mother had not violently opposed it, would have named his only son Lenin – had often said that the country was fast going to the dogs. Many of his friends were war-veterans, and he always started arguments with them by declaring that things were better when it was Rhodes who stood at the same intersection, also gazing northward.

"Sure," he would say, "I wasn't allowed to walk on the curb and the only day I was allowed near the bloody statue was on Pioneer Day when we were forced to play *'Rise O Voices of Rhodesia'* while the whites celebrated another successful year of subduing the natives. And I never forget the day an overzealous dog ruined my new suit at the Trade Fair, nor the fact that we couldn't be promoted to any positions of real power. But I will tell you one thing, man. I never went to bed on water and amagwadla back then! I saved up and bought all the furniture in my house! Because the economy made sense! And even if I couldn't walk on the pavement, the bloody streets were clean and vending in town was unheard of!"

Lungile swallowed a hard lump at the memory of his late father. The old geezer had been right and no one had paid him any attention. Lungile was hard pressed to remember the last time he had been able to buy anything worthwhile. The streets had not been re-tarred in years and in many places the potholes made walking beside the street a dangerous affair. Cars would turn in any direction just to avoid them. The pavements teemed with black faces, but merely because they had to sell fruits, vegetables and any other small items to put food on the table for that night.

He shook his head and walked on. Samantha's lunch break was only thirty minutes and he didn't want to miss it. She worked at a restaurant at the old department store on Fifteenth and what Lungile still referred to as Main Street. The work kept her mind off things and he was grateful for it, though sometimes he had to fight back the tears when she offered to buy him stuff on her meagre salary. She was a special girl. Lungile smiled.

They had been together since one rainy day three years before. He was on his way home from a Calculus exam that he knew he had failed. She wore a long red dress. The sky had been dark for some time and the rain had come suddenly. They had all but fallen over each other in their rush to hide in a disused doorway. The rain came down for the longest time that day and by the time they left they were chatting away like old friends.

She liked indie pop just like he did. They were both huge fans of Fun and even though some people may have found the lyrics depressing she thought their songs were great because on a happy day you could enjoy the music, and on a sad one you could just relate to the words and be glad that you were not alone. She had not finished high school, and she expressed envy when he told her he was coming from a University exam. Her deadbeat father had disappeared, leaving her and her mother to take care of her younger siblings, so school had ceased to be an option right after O-level. She told him the saddest details about her life even though they had just met. When he thought back to that day now, Lungile believed he had begun to fall in love with her the minute they met. She brought sunshine into his world, and when she hugged him, he always felt as if all his problems would disappear. It was as if in each embrace every bit of the love they had in their hearts became one and lit up their souls. It was the purest bliss.

He arrived at the old building ten minutes before Samantha's lunch break began. He did not like to seem like the overbearing boyfriend, so he never went in to look for her. Instead he would stand across the street and send a Please-Call-Me to signal that he was waiting. He pulled out his box of Everest and took out one of the remaining three cigarettes. He would have to smoke half and save the rest for later. No point in being extravagant in hard times. He lit it and stared at the ancient department store. He had no clue who owned it, or when it was built, but looking at it always made him wonder if the restaurant made enough money to support the rest of the business. The restaurant always seemed to be busy, but the store below it looked like it had been stocked out of a 1990s renaissance warehouse. On one occasion he had walked past with his mother, who was getting close to her sixties, and even she had been surprised at how old the clothes looked.

Lungile checked the time again. He carefully put out his cigarette before replacing it in the box. He searched his trouser pockets for a mint and found one in his back pocket. He unwrapped it, threw it in his mouth, and promptly crushed it with his molars to mask the tobacco smell. He was a different young man when he met Samantha, and he had changed a lot since, but one thing he had failed to do was to quit smoking. The fact that she knew, however, was not a reason to stink of tobacco.

She came rushing out of the store at half past one exactly and he knew she was not going anywhere today. She had her hairnet and apron on. He crossed the street and met her at the corner of the building.

"Hey, you," he greeted her with a smile.

She returned his smile and they hugged. When they pulled back, they kept their arms around each other's waists.

"How's your day going?" she inquired.

"Not bad. I've been all over town again today. Same story as always. 'We'll call you if anything comes up.'"

Getting a job seemed impossible. Lungile had submitted CVs every chance he got and every time he was promised a call that never came.

"Shame hey," she said, "let's hope something comes up."

He smiled and thanked her. She could not stay long because it was a busy day and two of the other girls had not shown up for work. They hugged again before he let her go.

One day, he thought as he watched her go back inside, *I will make this girl the queen of the world.*

When she was gone, he took off his backpack and rummaged through it for his earphones. He did not own a smart phone, but last year one of his oldest expat friends had sent him a second-generation eBook reader as a gift. It doubled as a music player, and since it did not fit in his pockets, he put all the songs he had on a playlist and concealed it in his backpack. He had made a hole at the top of the bag through which his earphones came out. He played Lovemore Majaivana's hit song *Umoya Wami*, then zipped up the bag, slung it over his shoulders, and put on his earphones. It was undoubtedly one of his favourite songs, and he enjoyed singing along. The opening lyrics of the song told a story of how Majee missed his hometown: Bulawayo. KoNtuthuziyathunqa – the place of billowing smoke.

As he ambled towards Belmont, Lungile wondered if the city still deserved this moniker. In the days when the song was released, the city was the country's industrial hub and it was because of this that it got its nickname. There was no billowing smoke now. Most companies had left for the capital city or simply given up. Belmont was deserted. A few of the premises opened on Sundays for those churches that could afford to rent space for their services. It seemed as if churches were the new industry. It was a pity that they only fed the mouths of the pastors and their families. Lungile was deep in thought when the aroma of freshly baked biscuits wafted into his nostrils. He smiled. Lobel's was one of the few resilient companies that remained. He remembered his mother telling him stories of how, when she worked for a textile company in her youth, she and a few other workmates would sit out on the grass in front of the bakery and inhale until they were full. She called it the Famous Lobel's Air-pie. He had visited Lobel's with his CV before. The lady at the reception had simply taken his envelope and thanked him. There was no promise of a call, and none was received. Lungile kept walking.

His music player was set to shuffle, and when *Umoya Wami* ended the next song brought a complete change. Twenty-One Pilots. Another of his favourites. He bobbed his head to the lyrics as he continued his excursion into the country's most famous ghost town. He had done the rounds before, each time carefully selecting companies where he saw even the slightest sign of activity. It was hard to tell sometimes. Even some of the ones that were still functional seemed deserted from afar, with weeds commandeering the driveway along with the rest of the premises. He always knew if a place was deserted because there would be trees growing where they would not normally be allowed to, and there were locks on the gates that looked older than Lungile cared to imagine.

He stopped just outside what was once The Standard Chartered Bank in Belmont. The bank had moved out of the building long ago, yet those who travelled by public transport still asked to be dropped off at Standard. Though the lettering had been removed the words 'Standard Chartered' were permanently tattooed on the faded wall. On the wall nearest the door hung a smaller sign for whatever company had moved in. Lungile opened the door and let himself in. The new company had not bothered to redesign the inside. You could still see the booths where the tellers should have been. Only the back offices where occupied. A short man in an old-fashioned summer shirt sat in the first office. He was struggling to stay awake behind his computer and he jumped up at the sight of Lungile, glad to have a customer to serve. He grinned ear to ear and shook Lungile's hand vigorously when he greeted him.

"Good afternoon, Sir. I've come to leave my CV."

The short man's grin did not fade. He reached out for the envelope, "Let me see!"

His eyes darted from left to right and back again as he perused Lungile's documents. He seemed to be enjoying himself and Lungile waited patiently for a few minutes.

"Ahaaa!" he said when he was done, "You I.T. boys! You want to come here and start blocking everything huh?"

Lungile chuckled and assured Summer-Shirt that he had no desire to block anything. He just wanted to work. Summer-Shirt was not convinced. He told Lungile about an I.T. Manager he had worked with at another company that had since closed.

"You should have seen Mrs Ncube's little boy – that's what we called him when he wasn't around. He was such a nuisance! Everything was linked to his machine and one time I saw a guy's machine switch off right in the middle of a video he was showing me on the internet. When he switched it on again it wouldn't log him in. Turned out the poor bastard had been fired!" He laughed before continuing, "Anyway, Mrs Ncube's little boy blocked everything. We couldn't even play CDs and for the longest time we weren't allowed to access the internet."

Lungile laughed and smiled respectfully. You never knew who you were talking to, so you had to be as polite as possible. Eventually Summer-Shirt put Lungile's CV in the IN tray on his desk and said the company would call if anything came up.

"Story of my life!" Lungile muttered as he walked back onto the street. He put his earphones on then promptly took them off again. The song that was playing was a sad one in which a woman asked her son if he would take care of her when his father was gone. Lungile's own father had passed away years ago, and the lyrics stung him because he was unable to take care of his mother. There was no point in depressing himself further. Instead he lit the cigarette he had stubbed earlier and walked on, ignoring the sun's heat. He had already sweated through his shirt, and he was sure he stunk, but he had to go on. He still had a lot of envelopes in his backpack. He knew he would be hearing a lot more promises of calls that would not come but it was better to try than to sit around feeling sorry for himself.

Three hours, two and a half cigarettes later he came to an old meat processing company's office at the end of Dullop Road in Donnington. By then he was low on energy. He had been all over Belmont and Donnington dropping CVs wherever he saw people. Earlier he had been impressed by how well taken care of the premises at Delta Beverages were and he was secretly hoping they would be the one company that called him. He had one last envelope in his backpack and after he dropped it he would make his way back into town to meet Samantha after she knocked off.

His shoes were covered in dust. Some of it had soiled the legs of his trousers up to the shin. He would have to wash them when he got home. He pulled the envelope out of his bag as he approached the gate. The yard was well kept. An old security guard sat in the cubicle just inside. Lungile greeted the old man, who stood up and approached the gate, his face a mask of curiosity.

"Hello, young man, how can I assist you?" he inquired.

Lungile told the old man he was looking for work. The old man looked at him and smiled ruefully.

"Let me show you something," he said, before disappearing into his cubicle.

Lungile waited. The old man reappeared carrying an old office dustbin. It was made of metal and it reminded Lungile of the ones his former schoolteachers kept near their desks. It was full of envelopes and sheets of used bond paper.

The old man rummaged through the bin's contents as he spoke, "These are all the CVs that have come in this month. I've watched kids like you bring them in, and I've seen these thrown away the very same day. I doubt anyone even opens them."

He pulled out three envelopes that were still sealed and held them out to Lungile.

"You see? I don't want to lie to you, and I don't want to waste your time. There is nothing here."

Lungile was dumbstruck. Some of the CVs in the bin bore the logos of the biggest universities in the country, the one he had attended among them. He stared at the old man.

"Why do you want a job anyway?" the guard asked. Lungile had not found his tongue, so the old man continued, "Let me show you something else."

He returned to his cubicle and brought out an old copy of *Farmer's Weekly*. It had seen better days but was still intact. On the cover there was a man in green overalls standing next to a huge ox. He looked very pleased with himself. The guard flipped through the magazine until he found the page he wanted, and then he held it up and showed it to Lungile.

"Tell me, son, what do you see here?"

Lungile looked at the picture, then back at the guard.

"Take your time and look," the old man encouraged, slightly waving the magazine.

He was looking at a dry veld. The grass had been burnt almost black by the sun. A few zebras, along with a foal, stood in a clearing in the middle of the veld. Lungile stared at the picture. Out of the corner of his eye he could see the guard smiling encouragingly at him. He scanned the picture from left to right; up and down. He had almost given up when he finally saw it.

"There is a lion in the grass! Right behind the zebras!"

The old guard laughed. He flipped through the pages and when he found what he was looking for he smiled, then he looked up and asked, "Where do you come from?"

"My people come from Plumtree," Lungile told him.

"Excellent, young man from Plumtree! Sometimes in life you must look beyond the obvious. And fortunately for you Plumtree is a great area for this."

He had opened a page with various pictures of goats, and he held the magazine up to Lungile again.

"If it's money you want, young man from Plumtree, this is the way to do it," he tapped a particularly plump goat with his index finger and fixed his eyes on Lungile. "The problem with you young guys is that you all want to be the big boss in some office job but there is so much more! How much does a goat cost?"

Lungile did not know, but he speculated that it might cost around sixty dollars.

"And how much does it cost to raise one?" the old man asked.

Again, Lungile did not know.

The old man smiled patiently and continued, "Let's assume you buy a goat at sixty dollars like you say. If you buy a male and a female goat, they will cost you a hundred and twenty. Now, that is quite a bit of money, but who ever started a business for free? Anyway, once you have your two goats, young man from Plumtree, you can breed these and raise them at a relatively low cost, considering all the grassland in your home area, right?"

Lungile nodded slowly and the old man spoke again.

"Obviously you would need vaccines and maybe every now and then you might want to buy specialised feed, but a goat's gestation period is about five months. Think how many goats you would have in a few years. All for the cost of two goats, and you would be selling them, as you said, at around sixty dollars, wouldn't you? What do you think?"

He shut his book and eyed Lungile. Lungile said nothing. Up to that point he had never thought about anything like that and it was difficult for him to come up with a response. The old man was still smiling.

"Everything you need to make money in this world, young man from Plumtree, is right at your fingertips. You just have to look."

They stood and chatted a few minutes more. The old man came from Matopos. He had worked on farms for most of his life but was forced to leave that profession behind when the economy took a nosedive. His sons were in South Africa, but he had to find work as a guard to support his wife and a couple of younger daughters. He had begun to raise goats at his rural home in Matopos, and he hoped that soon he could leave this life behind. But for now he would keep on working.

Eventually Lungile had to bid him farewell. He could not afford to linger any longer. The old man wished him luck and returned to his cubicle, where he sat down and continued to read his magazine with a smile on his face. Lungile put on his earphones as he walked away. His music player had found its way back to *Umoya Wami*. He stopped and pulled the eBook reader out of his bag. He put it on repeat and continued on his way. He thought about the old security guard as he re-joined the road that connected Bulawayo and Plumtree, his father's hometown. He sang along, wishing he had saved his last cigarette for the walk back into town.

LAYERS

Brown woke up feeling how much she had aged in the years since she first awoke inside the glass cage. Her back ached in a million places. It wasn't the first time she thought about the queen-sized bed she left at home. This straw bed was a serious downgrade, but it beat sleeping on the floor, and it came in handy every six or so months when she had to lay an egg.

The cage was designed – as much as possible – to look like a flat. A cosy flat with no partitions between the rooms. She lay on her straw bed at the back of the room. To her left was the shower. Next to that was the toilet. From the foot of the bed came what was supposed to be the living room, and that was as far as the illusion went. There was no kitchen. Her food was delivered through a tube and onto a trough to the left of the living room area. The menu usually consisted of dried fruits, fresh vegetables, and – occasionally – snails.

Brown forced herself to get up and then hobbled toward the trough now. The day's rations had already been released and that meant she'd slept almost long enough to miss the daily visit from her captors. It was a pity she was awake now and would have to watch the whole thing again. She scooped up a few dried apple slices and went to stand by the glass window at the front of her grand room.

The cages stretched as far as her eyes could see. Inside there were humans of varying ages and ethnicities. She had not been outside the cage since her arrival years before and it seemed to Brown as if she'd spent her entire life in captivity. The last thing she remembered from her life before this place was the day she went to Mater Dei Hospital for her hormone implant.

She had never heard of epigenetic markers before the giants arrived. As far as she knew a man and a woman had sex, the woman fell pregnant, and nine months later a baby was born. She never really bothered to find out the science behind how the giants knew how to bypass the sexual intercourse, but less than six months after the first exchanges between the humans and the giants, epigenetic markers were trending all over the internet. Brown was one of many who were excited that they could finally have children without worrying about marriage or commitment. She especially latched on to a phrase from an article she read which stated that people of any gender could now 'produce the necessary markers for them to reproduce asexually without any genetic deficiencies impairing the child.'

Brown went for it without hesitation. She had suffered through various romantic disasters, including the college sweetheart who lost his courage on their wedding day and never showed up for the ceremony. That was the last straw. She gave up on love and lived alone, secretly angry at men for not loving her and for denying her the joys of motherhood. At last, at age thirty-three, she was happy to have found a way to have children on her own without the unrealistic costs of insemination.

Now Brown staggered back to the straw bed and looked at the egg she had laid last night. It was her sixty-fourth but laying it had hurt as much as the first time. She picked it up and hugged it. She never got to keep any of them, and as a result she felt a hunger that she was sure would never be satisfied. She could live a thousand lifetimes and never recover from the grief of all the children she lost. She had considered destroying the eggs, but she could not bring herself to do it. Now she lay down next to the egg and fell asleep whispering promises that she knew she could not keep.

The giant doors opened much later than Brown anticipated. Her captors ambled in. They were slow creatures. The older one had fur all over his body, while the younger was completely hairless. From afar they could be mistaken for giant men, but as they got closer any similarities to humanity disappeared. Their eyes were dark sockets that were barely separated by a section of flesh. Their noses could be missed entirely if one did not have the privileged view from inside one of the cages. Brown hated looking at their faces. The flat noses especially made her skin want to crawl off her flesh.

Now the giants shuffled along the passages between the hundreds of cages. Brown was right about one thing, the cages stretched on far beyond her sight. The room was much larger than she would ever see from within her cage. And the cages were arranged in neat little rows so that the giants could get between them and collect whatever they needed to collect without expending too much effort.

When they finally got to Brown's cage, the older giant stopped and peered inside. Brown averted her face. She moved to the living area and studied the floor as if she had not been looking at it now for what must have been over twenty years. She never knew how many people were imprisoned here in these cages, but she knew that the giants carried large baskets for the eggs. All they had to do was open the top of the cage and push her aside. She loathed them, but she was helpless.

The cages only ever opened for one other reason: Death. She recalled the morning, years ago now, when she woke up to find that her neighbour had died at some point during the night. Rigor mortis was not done arranging the poor woman's limbs, but there was no mistaking it. When the giants found her, they opened the neighbouring cage, picked up the slowly stiffening woman by her leg, and took her away. It was a few weeks before a new occupant was placed in the cage. It was a teenage boy. Brown sensed something vaguely familiar about the young man, but she knew she could never have met him before. Although her hair was shorter and blacker, she had been the giants' captive too long by then to know any teenagers personally. Now the teenager was a handsome young man; probably in his thirties, and as she remembered his arrival, Brown wondered if he had ever known freedom at all.

She was shocked back to the present when she felt the giant's hairy hands grabbing her. Had she been younger, she might have struggled, but now she allowed herself to be picked up. The giants could snap her like a twig if they so wished. If anyone had been observing, it would have been like watching a man pick up a baby. A fully developed baby with breasts and pubic hair to boot. The giant brought her close to its face and sniffed. Once. Twice. Brown closed her eyes tight before she heard it say something to the younger one in that garbled gibberish that they used to communicate.

"Gor vim vim!" the younger one said, nodding.

Brown was struck with fear. Instead of being returned to the cage her arms were bound to her sides, then she was put inside a smaller cage. This one was clearly designed for conveyance. The younger giant picked up this cage and walked behind the older one as it continued to harvest eggs from the other cages.

For the first time Brown got to see just how large the room was. She was shocked by the length of the passage that had been her neighbourhood all these years, and even more so by the fact that the room was almost as wide as it was long, with rows separating the cages so the giants could walk between them. The other captives, she saw, were mostly young people, certainly younger than her. Her gaze passed from one cage to the next, seeing expressionless teenagers, and a few angry looking older men and women. The younger ones just seemed resigned to the fact that all they could do was feed on bits of fruit and lay eggs for the giants to collect. They simply watched as the eggs were taken away. Some of the older ones, the ones Brown thought might be closer to her age, tried to fight the giants. It was a futile effort.

As they approached the door, Brown locked eyes with a young woman and felt the strength go out of her knees. The young woman stared back with no life in her eyes. She had long black hair that stood like wildfire on her head. Brown marked the familiar shape of the body, and the complexion that had earned her the nickname 'Black Beauty' in high school. Save for that dead look in her eyes, Brown could have been looking in a mirror. One that allowed you to look back in time. And in that moment, kneeling in the moving cage, she realized what she had not known all these years. Some of her children were in here with her all along. Her young neighbour's face swam back into view. She remembered his nose. His eyes that she should have recognized instantly. Hadn't she been teased by her friend Tasha in high school for those eyes? She could almost hear her long-forgotten friend's laughter between comments about the size of her eyes. Silently, Brown began to weep. If she had known better, she would have saved her tears for later.

At last they stepped through the main door. Bright light dazzled her. She could not remember the last time she had seen the sun. When her eyes finally cleared, she looked around. The dust on the ground below her was green. Without a closer look, one might have mistaken it for moss. For the most part the trees in the distance looked like normal trees, until you saw that all of them had magenta leaves.

Her heart now danced on her tongue. She still shed tears silently, but her mind had moved on to more immediate questions. Had she ever seen anyone taken out of their cage alive? She didn't think she had. She had only seen that dead neighbour of hers. What was happening? If her high school English teacher had been around to comment on her thoughts, he would have told her that there was only one way to find out. And it was not as if she had a choice. Brown simply looked on, unable to wipe the tears on her face, as she was carried away from the cages she had come to think of as her final home in life.

A large house-like shape loomed into view. As they got closer, Brown noted that it was indeed a house. It was like nothing she had ever seen before. Made entirely of stone, it looked as if someone had found a giant boulder and sculpted a house out of it. When they stepped inside, she marvelled at the furniture inside. It was also made of stone, and she couldn't help wondering how the giants had crafted it.

She felt the cage rise and saw she was being placed on a table top. There were giant knives on the table and a large bowl filled with what Brown could only assume was fruit from this strange place. The older giant counted five eggs out of the basket and then spoke to the young one again.

"Timin ababala fa," or something like that, it said, and then picked up the basket and walked away.

The younger one reached under the table and brought out a large stone bowl. Brown watched in horror as it bit a hole in the membrane of one egg. When this was accomplished, it squeezed an off-white fluid into the bowl. Brown's chest constricted as it picked up another egg and again bit a hole in its membrane and squeezed the contents into the bowl. Somewhere far away, an old woman began to scream. It had been years since she had spoken to anyone, and she was screaming for minutes before she realised that the voice was hers. She struggled against the ropes in vain. The young giant turned its vacant black eyes to her and looked at her, and then carried on emptying the eggs into the bowl. Brown screamed herself hoarse and carried right on screaming; a rasping, quiet sound of no consequence.

One thought replayed itself continuously: *BREEDING AND BREAKFAST OH MY GOD THEY DON'T BREED ALL OF THEM SOME OF MY CHILDREN ARE BREAKFAST!*

Eventually the screaming and struggling wore her out. All the while the younger giant had not only destroyed the eggs, but it had gone on to beat them, and then pour them onto a skillet at the far end of the room and cook them. Brown sat in her cage dazed. She didn't struggle when it turned its attention to her. Her mind was someplace else. Someplace back home. In Bulawayo. Somewhere *secret.* Someplace where alien giants didn't cook human eggs. Her children. Never mind the other captives! These monsters had spent all these years *cooking* her children!

She stared into space as the giant opened the portable cage and picked her up. She remained still as it untied her and inspected her ancient body before laying her down on the table. She didn't see it grab a much bigger knife from somewhere under that large table. In those final moments, lying on the table with her mind trying frantically to protect the last bit of her sanity, Brown had one final thought before the giant brought the knife down hard on her neck: If her eggs were breakfast, what were they going to do to her?

GOODNIGHT, AUFIDIUS

It had become the ritual every weekend. Thinking he shouldn't be drinking on an empty stomach, Nkathazo sat at Thaba Nchu Lodge with his friend Xolani, slowly sipping on free booze. Xolani was formally employed at ZESA. His pockets were perpetually full and Nkathazo was often the sole beneficiary of his generosity, especially when beer was involved.

The lodge was busy. On Saturday afternoons parents brought their kids here to play in the pool or on the trampoline while they sat in the garden and enjoyed a few drinks. To Nkathazo it seemed like the perfect way to keep your wife from nagging about spending time with her and the family. Maybe one day he could copy the technique.

Xolani exploded into a series of expletives. A player whose name Nkathazo didn't know had fired a shot high over the bar on the TV. It was Liverpool versus Arsenal. Nkathazo's interest in football had waned in the years since the World Cup in South Africa. Back then he was the epitome of a fanatic. He'd kept track of every single game in an exercise book. If you wanted to know who'd scored or earned himself a red card, Nkathazo would have been the one to tell you. But now he couldn't have cared less. The outings served merely as a way to get out and see people and, naturally, to have the drinks he often couldn't afford to pay for himself. He stood up and stretched.

"I need a smoke," he announced.

Xolani kept his eyes on the TV. Nkathazo walked out of the tiny thatched hut that served as the bar and walked towards the gate. The sun was a bright red dot in the west. He pulled out his box of cigarettes and mentally noted that he was two smokes away from desperation before he fumbled for one and stuck it in his mouth. His phone vibrated in his pocket. He pulled it out and read the text.

Hme alne 2nyt. Wna cum?

He smiled, and then took a long drag of his cigarette as he texted back.

Blink 317 times and I'll be there.

Her response came within seconds.

K ☺

Nkathazo finished his cigarette, still smiling. Back in the bar he showed Xolani the text.

"Who's Rumbi?"

"That's need-to-know, general," Nkathazo chuckled.

Xolani laughed excitedly, "Ok, let's go. Bro, for pussy I can even drive you there myself!"

They downed their drinks and left in Xolani's old Mazda B1800. The car had seen better days. It belonged to Xolani's father before his ancestors called him to the mountain. Xolani loved it like a sibling even though it coughed and sputtered as if it would just die forever in the middle of the road. Still, the old gal had power in her engine. The duo covered the gap between Thaba Nchu and Nkathazo's house in under ten minutes.

"If you make it quick, I'll drive you to the bus stop!" Xolani shouted as Nkathazo opened the gate.

Nkathazo all but ran to his backyard room. He showered as quickly as he could (which is to say he ran the water, stepped under it, quickly rubbed his armpits and genitals, then stepped out) and then found a fresh pair of jeans and a t-shirt. He opened the pot of rice he had left on his single plate stove then decided against eating. He could always do that later.

Instead of driving Nkathazo to the bus stop at the end of the street, Xolani drove him to Leeside filling station. It was a huge favour. Getting transport in Manningdale was difficult. One could spend close to an hour without a single kombi showing up. In this neighbourhood transport cars were a dime a dozen. If you spent ten minutes without seeing a Honda Fit looking for passengers then you weren't paying attention. Xolani pulled up at the bus stop and grinned at Nkathazo.

"You lucky bastard! Shouldn't be hard to get to town from here, man."

Nkathazo thanked him and got out of the car. The sun had kissed the horizon already. He would probably get to Rumbi's house after dark.

He muttered, "Shit."

A red Honda stopped in front of him and he jumped in. The tiny car vibrated with the sounds of South African house music. It sped off towards the city centre as soon as he got in. Nkathazo had to resist the urge to hold on to the passenger next to him. When they got to town, the streetlights were already on. August sunsets came with a suddenness that Nkathazo couldn't get used to. He dropped off at the city's main mall and made his way towards the corner of Eleventh Avenue and Fort Street, where he would find transport to Newton West. He would have to brave the two kilometres from the end of Derby Road to Rumbi's house in the dark.

He shrugged and thought, *No pain, no game.*

Town was busy. Schools were due to reopen the following Tuesday and all the high school kids were on the loose, making the most of their last weekend of freedom. Many of them were stone drunk already. A young girl had passed out near the Western Union Office on Tenth Avenue. She couldn't have been a day over fifteen. She lay sprawled next to a pool of vomit. Two worried-looking girls – presumably her friends – stood watching as the boys they were with tried in vain to wake her up. He shook his head and made his way through the sea of teenagers.

He stopped at an Inns Express along Fort Street to buy condoms. It was always an uncomfortable experience. In this case even more so because the only cashier in the store was a woman old enough to be his grandmother. He walked reluctantly toward her, carefully avoiding eye contact. He picked up a pack of Piccadilly mints before he stepped up to the till and requested a pack of regular Protector Plus. He could have been imagining it, but he was sure the old woman smiled mischievously as she rang up the items and handed him his change. Back outside he popped a mint into his mouth.

Before long, he was at Derby Road. It was deserted and there were no streetlights. He walked in the moon's scant light. His only comfort was that there wasn't a lot of traffic in this neighbourhood. Any thieves who came here would have been looking for a fantastic way to waste their time. Still he walked straight down the middle of the road, ignoring thoughts about how ominously the dark shapes of what he knew to be mostly acacia trees seemed to be reaching out toward him. He recited his favourite audition monologue to keep calm.

"O Marcius, Marcius!" he recited to the trees, *"Each*
word thou hast spoke hath weeded from my heart
A root of ancient envy…"

He still remembered the words from the production of *Coriolanus* in high school, and he always went to that section whenever he was asked to recite something at an audition. He was close to the end of the full speech when he arrived at Rumbi's gate. It was open.

He stepped in and, as always, he admired the garden. It was well lit. The grass was evergreen, and the gnomes happily stood guard around the giant birdbath in the middle. His phone buzzed in his pocket. He looked at the message and smiled.

U cn admire e nomes in e mrng.

He went to the door and knocked. Rumbi was always a sight for sore eyes. She opened the door in a dark-coloured nylon nightgown that went nearly all the way down to her ankles. Their hug confirmed what his eyes had already told him; she wore only the gown. She planted a kiss on his lips and led him to the living room.

After her welcome performance she brought him dinner and a cold glass of Mazoe Orange. They caught up while he ate. It had been a few months since their last booty call.

"How's the acting going?" she asked.

He responded through a mouthful of rice, "Still barely paying the bills."

He swallowed and had a sip of Mazoe.

"I'm doing a movie right now. It's called *Imbulu*." He put down his glass and said, "Guess what it's about."

She laughed, "I don't know. An uptight girl?"

He smiled and pushed a few grains of rice around his plate with his fork, "No. You ever heard the story of Imbul'makhasane?"

Rumbi shook her head.

"Really?" He chuckled.

She stared at him. No sign of recognition on her face whatsoever.

"It's a story about a princess who gets tricked by this … sort of… dragon woman," he said.

He loved explaining folklore. He knew a lot of people who had never heard the stories before.

"They meet in the bush when the young lady is on her way to get married to a king in the next village. The dragon woman plays on her good heart and tricks the girl into exchanging clothes with her. From there the dragon pretends to be the girl and she marries the king. The girl is relegated to the dragon woman's slave."

He took a bite of chicken. Fried chicken was never as good as when he ate it at Rumbi's house.

He continued, "Anyway, these guys are putting their own spin on the story. I'm playing the young king who unwittingly marries Imbul'makhasane."

Rumbi rubbed her elbow, "Sounds creepy."

"I know, right?"

There was a long silence.

He spoke first, "And you? How are things at the brewery?"

"Same shit, different day."

She rarely spoke about her job, and he didn't press for details. After dinner Nkathazo switched off his phone. His nights with Rumbi were always like stepping into another life and he didn't want reality interfering with it. She ran hot water in her huge bathtub.

She lived alone. Her siblings had all moved to the United Kingdom and her mother was never keen on living in the city. Occasionally, the old woman would visit to make sure the house wasn't falling apart. The rest of the time Rumbi had it all to herself. She kept it smart. Her bathroom smelt of oils and bath salts he had never even heard of until he met her. Her kitchen was a study in spices and herbs. Her bedroom could put some of the fanciest hotels to shame. She worked for the biggest manufacturer of alcohol in the country and her lifestyle showed how well it paid. After each visit to her house he felt like he'd been at a luxurious resort.

They stepped into the tub and washed each other delicately, slowly, like two lovers desperate to make the most of their time together before the spell wore off. His fingers traced her skin. He never tired of looking at her body. Her tiny waist accentuated her hips, made him think of Toni Braxton's *Spanish Guitar.*

She'd been dating a trucker since high school, and she only called Nkathazo when he was out of the country. From the way she spoke about him, Nkathazo could tell she had grown tired of him and wanted something new. He didn't know if he was that something new, but he knew he could get used to this life. If only his heart could agree. He savoured their bath, eagerly anticipating what was to come.

In the bedroom she was everything a man could ever dream of. She never asked you to do things to her. She gave precise, direct instructions. You didn't sleep at Rumbi's house. You lost yourself in her. Your bodies would almost meld, determined to recreate Shakespeare's beast with two backs. Except in those moments it felt like a permanent state of being. Her mahogany skin glistened with sweat. Her screams and moans filled the room. You fucked until you thought you couldn't do it anymore but, still, you kept going because until she said stop, you couldn't.

*

When Nkathazo woke up the following morning, she was staring at him with a smile on her face.

"I missed that."

"Not as much as I did," he said.

She kissed him and got out of bed, "Time to get up, Sleeping Beauty."

They took a walk to the shops together. She never allowed him to leave without getting breakfast first. They bought eggs and rolls. She always asked if he needed anything for home. He always said no. She'd been to his place just once. She never asked to visit again. She'd been disappointed by his little rented room in Manningdale. She didn't have to say it; her eyes did all the talking. The room wasn't even half as big as her bathroom. Still he refused to let her think this was about money.

Back at the house they made breakfast together, which is to say she made omelettes and he boiled water and made idle conversation. After breakfast they cuddled on the sofa, watching *South African Idols* repeats and laughing at all the terrible singers that showed up to audition. At some point they fell asleep in each other's arms, smiling from each other's company.

*

A few days later Nkathazo was on set for *Imbulu*, chatting with the director. He was the first person to arrive. At first the director was livid. He listened quietly as she ranted about everyone else and the fact that they couldn't take the business seriously. After a few minutes she ran out of wind and just sat down, impatiently checking the production WhatsApp group to see if anyone had said anything.

"This is Africa," Nkathazo said, "Time is a made-up concept here. People treat it like a suggestion. You want people here on time? Tell them you're starting two hours before your actual call time."

She threw up her hands, "But we're African too and we're here!"

"Exception to the rule. To everyone else time can be bent to your will."

The conversation turned to all his previous work in the industry. She laughed when he told her about a film he'd done the previous year. The make-up artist put a little white paint along his hairline so he could play a forty-eight-year-old man. He laughed with her and said he was glad it wasn't released. His phone interrupted the conversation. He frowned at the screen before answering.

"Sibongile. What a surprise."

"Aufidius, how are you?"

They met through *Coriolanus*. She played the wife of Marcius Caius. Ironically, the actor playing Caius was her boyfriend at the time. Nkathazo played Tullus Aufidius. His chemistry with Sibongile was off the charts, but she'd placed him firmly in the friend zone. Their friendship had lasted long after the play, but after a while they drifted apart the way people do when the magic of the production has worn off. For close to ten years he didn't see her. Then a couple of years ago he bumped into her at the Intwasa Arts Festival.

"Could be better," he said now.

She laughed, "Come now, Aufidius. Surely you can show a little more enthusiasm."

He smiled, "I'm doing just fine, Sibo. I'm just wondering what the special occasion is."

"Surely an old friend can look you up when she's in town, can't she?"

He could almost picture the look on her face as she spoke. At Intwasa they had caught each other up on what was happening in their lives. She was single, employed by the government and earning enough to keep a house in Bulawayo and another in Harare. The exact nature of her job remained a secret. He was still chasing the dream, trying to make it big as an actor. They exchanged numbers and from then on, whenever she got lonely, she would call him. But they had not spoken in months. All his texts since had gone unanswered.

He said nothing.

"Are you still there, Aufidius?"

"Yeah, I'm just wondering if this isn't some grand hallucination," he said, "You kinda went cold on me… Virgilia."

"Well, you know how it is when you work for The Man," she paused, and he heard what sounded like her sipping on a drink, "Maybe I can make it up to you this Friday?"

"Maybe you can," he found himself smiling again.

"So... Dinner and drinks?" she asked, and then continued before he could answer, "You still like that bar opposite The Bulawayo

Sun?"

"Yes," he chuckled, "And you still insist on calling it The Bulawayo Sun?"

"They shouldn't have changed it to that lame ass new name to begin with."

Nkathazo smiled after the call. He did miss having intelligent conversations. Drinks sounded like fun and he would have shot the last of his scenes in *Imbulu* by then so maybe he'd have a bit of currency himself. Not that it mattered. When people knew you were an artist it was as if they felt compelled to pay for everything.

*

They met at the Safari Bar as agreed. She came clad in tight black jeans and a blouse cut low enough to be sexy but high enough to still be classy. He was in a tracksuit. His final shoot had been postponed to Friday. There wasn't enough time for him to go home and change. She ordered wine. He bought a Castle Lager.

"So, what is Aufidius up to lately?"

"Same old same old," he smiled and sipped his beer.

"Acting still?"

"Why does everyone ask that like I'm some kind of mental patient?"

"Well, you know how it is in this country, don't you?"

He raised his eyebrows, "How it is?"

She laughed and touched her upper lip with the tip of her tongue and then said, "Look at the Gringos of this world. All that fame and nothing to show for it."

"First of all, I wouldn't call it fame. And second, I'm not Lazarus Boora!"

"Well I can see you haven't lost your passion for it," she said.

She finished her wine and motioned for the waitress to bring another. Nkathazo pointed at his bottle and gave the waitress the peace sign. After finishing the rest of his beer, he said, "You make it sound like I have a choice."

"But you do!"

"Oh, here it comes."

He rolled his eyes and dramatically put a hand to his forehead.

"Joke all you want, Aufidius, but you have a degree that you could use to benefit this country!" she said.

Sometimes talking to Sibongile was draining. She never shut up about how talented he was and what he could do for the country. It came from a good place. He had a talent for mathematics and a degree to support it. A lot of the people from his class lived in big houses and drove fancy cars. If you knew all the right people a degree could open doors that others had spent years trying to unlock. And he knew Sibo. But she never seemed to understand how excruciating university had been for him. He'd known since high school that he wanted to be an actor. Convincing his parents had been equally hard. So, he'd done what they wanted. It was their money after all. When he was done, he put his degree in a suitcase along with his few clothes and left home. His mother still called every once in a while, to try and talk sense into him. His father, at least, had come around eventually. The last time they had seen each other the old man had told him he always wanted to be a singer, but he'd never had the courage to stand up to everyone who said it was a poor man's endeavour.

Nkathazo hated having this conversation with Sibo.

"Can we change the subject?"

She must have seen something in his eyes. Ordinarily she would have teased him awhile longer. This time she drank her wine.

"How about we move the party to my place?" she asked with a crooked smile.

"I've never said no to that before," he said, smiling back.

Later, she drove him to his house. She never allowed him to sleep over. He'd never asked why, although a part of him sensed she didn't want to get too attached. She treated him like a plaything, teased incessantly, poked at his sore spots. But outside of that they had the best conversations. In all the time he had known her it was the one thing that kept him from losing interest in her. Sometimes they'd talk even as they kissed and undressed each other. She touched him delicately and hugged him hard. Her kisses lingered. He didn't like to think about the only other person who had kissed him like that. She belonged in the past.

At his gate Sibo turned off the engine and sighed.

"So, you'd really rather have this than a real relationship?" he asked.

"Are you ready to commit?" She turned to him and raised an eyebrow, "To let go of your silly childish dreams?"

He opened the door and got out. Then he peered in at her and said, "Goodnight, Sibo."

"Goodnight," she replied. Then after a pause, "Aufidius."

IN THE SHADOWS

The dark mountains in the west were swallowing Mvelinqangi's red orb when I checked into my room. I swiped my key card on the door and wondered if being alone was always part of the hotel experience. The room was silent, restored to life only when the maidBot's motion sensors activated its welcome sequence.

"A sunny welcome to –"

"Deactivate," I commanded.

The clumsy contraption backed into its charging port and the low hum in its chest died down as the motors went off. A few seconds later the lights in its eyes faded. The only thing I hated more than these field assignments was the way robots had taken over all aspects of customer service. I longed for the days when hotel receptions meant a warm smile; when one wondered if the room service personnel were as pleasant to all the other guests.

The room was as a hotel room should be. A bed made with clean white sheets and a dull coloured throw – grey in this case – neatly rolled up at its foot; a Gideon's Bible on the nightstand; teacups and a kettle next to it. The dying colours of the day shone through the window. The street below bustled with activity. To the east it led to affluent suburbs and the mystic highlands. To the west it led into the heart of the state. As a result, the middle choked with traffic. In the section below the hotel people waited to be ferried to different destinations. Low cost transport cars that The Union manufactured in the upper west weaved in and out of the merciless flow of traffic. Touts hung from their doors harassing anyone who was going to a destination other than the one on offer.

My thoughts turned to Thoko. She was killed in a hotel room a lot like this one. At least that was what the report said. In the years leading up to the formation of The Union she had won various awards for her fearless journalism. When the conflict erupted in the former Democratic Republic of the Congo, she was one of the first to be assigned there. The opportunity excited her. She was eager to cover the stories of how the rebel forces were surviving the harsh war. Rebels. She taught me a different way of looking at the word. The whole world called them that because the news called them that. In Thoko's stories they became human beings. They were fathers of children who dreamt of careers in medicine. They were boys whose mothers obsessively inspected their sheets to make sure they were not masturbating. There was a story behind every individual in every picture. In one she stood with an enormous man whose grin lit up the whole scene. His face was riddled with the markings of a pugilist's life. He would die an undefeated champion, but the war had forever robbed him of his most valuable tools. In the picture he held an AK in his remaining hand.

In the end it wasn't the men resisting the system who killed her. It wasn't even those protecting it. The investigation revealed that the doorman at the hotel where she turned scraps of notes into articles was a depraved animal. She was repatriated headless, with her genitals mutilated and gaping holes where her supple breasts once stood. Her body's failure to produce melanin had doomed her to a painful death for the sake of some madman's potion. My work with The Shadow eventually landed me in the DRC years later. It was called a personal favour to me. And no questions were asked when I returned.

The room materialised before my eyes again. How long had I stood by the window? Barely ten minutes according to the watch on my wrist. I decided against going to the downstairs bar for a drink.

"And besides," I said to the empty room, "there's enough work to be done here."

I sat down on the bed. Memories of Thoko were only a distraction. That life was a long time ago. I opened my suitcase and dumped its contents on the bed. I picked up the bottle of Jack Daniels I had carefully packed in the middle. A gift from an old friend. He'd given it to me the day he retired. I tried to refuse. I should have been the one giving him gifts. But he insisted.

"I've had enough liquor to last me a lifetime," he'd argued.

I smiled at the bottle and his voice came from my lips, echoing his last words to me.

"Let's hope the good guys will keep winning."

I stashed the bottle in the small safe in the closet and set a new unlock code. The time to open it had not yet come. It would come when the job was done.

A loud knock interrupted my thoughts.

Thoko was one of the good guys. But people like her never win. Winning should have meant changing the lives of her readers so much that the world swore off fighting wars. At least that was how I saw it when I was younger. Before The Shadow and greying hair.

The man at the door saw things differently. In his world there were no good guys and bad guys. Just winners and losers. He often boasted that he had never sided with losers in his life. We had fought many wars together. Some at home. Some overseas. Everywhere. On the surface we were a loudmouth from Luveve and a belligerent bumpkin from Vengere. Behind closed doors we were a formidable combination of brute force and strategy. When The Union was young we had both been recruited to The Shadow for our brilliant service to our now obsolete country. Once there we had quickly proved our value. And yet even as we approached retirement age, we still found ourselves being put on field assignments.

GM held out a tray bearing a wine bucket and two glasses. Long Mountain Red. 2008. He was masquerading as my bodyguard.

"I hope you like the room, Sir."

"Very much, thanks, Gwenyambira."

He grinned, and then dropped me a naughty wink, "So you insist on pleasure before business, huh?"

I shrugged.

GM knew about my trysts with Nyararai each time I came to Gutaguru. There was no point in hiding it from him.

"Umsebenz' aw'baleki, bhururu. She should be on her way already."

"Very good, Sir."

I bade him goodnight and shut the door. One of the perks of

working for The Shadow was that our work required us to be unmonitored. Any surveillance on operatives could lead to uncomfortable conversations later. So we were allowed to go dark. All that mattered was completing the mission. With all the travelling I did, my list of contacts had grown considerably over the years. I had friends in a lot of cities and Nyararai was one of them. In her eyes I was a suave businessman who looked her up whenever he was in the former capital of Zimbabwe. It was still one of The Union's most vibrant cities, home to all sorts of movers and shakers. Nyararai's political aspirations had brought her here soon after she graduated from University. Before university she was a rich girl who slummed it for a while in Bulawayo's high-density suburbs and came out of it a better member of society. Trust fund restored, she began a crusade to build a better world for all young people.

"We can't repeat the mistakes of history. We can't just tell girls 'Here you go, this is freedom!' without teaching the boys not to be chauvinist in their thinking."

She also did her own fair share of travelling, particularly in the rural areas. Her team was made up of various professionals whose goal was to help her make sure all the children they encountered understood that their options went beyond civil service.

She let herself in when she arrived. I was in the shower savouring the feeling of hot water drumming against my head and shoulders, tension melting away beneath my muscles. Nyararai could be deadly silent when she wanted. She is still the only person who ever managed to sneak up on me. To the outside world, she was a hard case politician from the old school who didn't take no for an answer. She liked it that way. But within the walls of various rooms in various hotels, she was softer, the lines on her face less harsh. It was impossible not to return her smile.

We fucked like it was Armageddon. And afterwards she talked about those days in Sizinda, cut off from her father's wealth. He was the true hard case. He was in politics before the massive restructuring at The Union's inception. He kicked her out after he found out she was dating an unemployed boy of 'questionable heritage' from the high-density suburbs.

"It was just tribalism with extra steps," she said. Her head was on my chest, her fingers tracing the fading muscles on my abdomen. "My father had this deep-seated hatred of anyone who wasn't Zezuru. When he kicked me out, he told me I could come back when I had regained my senses."

But at 18, she had already seen more luxury than Mehluli – the boyfriend from Sizinda – ever would. Her life had been one of new cars every year, of holidays in hotels where the menus didn't list prices, of grown men kow-towing to her family and of overly eager customer service reps who called her 'mother' even though they were easily her seniors. Mehluli lived in a single room built at the back of his parents' yard to allow him some semblance of privacy after he had outgrown sharing a room with his little sisters. They spent many afternoons in that room. They lay on his single mattress and he told her how he wanted a better future for his own children. They had been lying in each other's arms when policemen armed with sledgehammers descended on the neighbourhood, destroying what they were calling illegal structures. The experiences in Sizinda woke her up.

In the morning I traced her greying locks with my fingers. She was significantly younger than me. She was approaching fifty but unlike other women her age she refused to walk around announcing it every chance she got. She would mimic them with disdain; holding on to her waist and walking like the next step could be her last.

"Ah sengimdala shuwa!"

She was committed to physical fitness. In her book a politician lost a little of the people's faith with every inch gained on her waist. Breasts that should have drooped long ago stood proudly on her chest, and her bottom was firm enough to put younger women to shame.

She stirred awake.

"Hey."

"Uvuke njani?" I whispered.

"Hungry." A mischievous smile spread across her lips.

"That we can fix."

When she climaxed, she called a name that was never mine. She would die not knowing it belonged to a man whose death certificate was written years before we ever met.

"Amos!" she screamed repeatedly.

After she left for work, I remained in the hotel room and worked on the maidBot. My weapons contact had given me precise instructions for rewiring it. The robot's eyes stared blankly ahead as I removed and reconnected various wires in its midsection. They were a remnant of twentieth century technology. Motorised limbs controlled with logic circuits. With some complex rewiring, its main processor would attempt to process a recursive loop that resulted in too much heat being generated in the power supply unit. A few minutes after that:

"Boom." I whispered.

When the work was done I went downstairs for lunch. I like to keep it simple. I ordered the Zim beef special: three hundred grams of beef and a modest helping of is'tshwala and spinach. There was also half a tomato sprinkled with black pepper. It looked as if the chef had added it as an afterthought. I ate slowly and watched the other patrons. Three old ladies sat a few tables in front of me. They were smoking and having quite an animated conversation in Italian. The oldest of them had a hoarse smoker's voice. I was convinced that on the phone she was often mistaken for a man. Behind them a group of French youths made fun of the waiter's attempts to greet them in their own language. He laughed along with them.

GM appeared like a spirit and sat down at the opposite end of my table.

"So, Tshisa."

He fixed his eyes on mine.

After a few seconds of silence, I responded, "That's not a full sentence."

He laughed, "Watanga, m'face wangu. Are we ready?"

I nodded.

"Good. I'll have the car ready before the cock crows tomorrow morning."

"I doubt you'll hear any cocks in this part of Harare, GM."

He grinned as he left the table, "Don't let The Head catch you using the old name!"

Back in my room I lay on the unmade bed and thought about Nyararai. My work with The Shadow had robbed me of every tear I could ever shed. I had been death's agent longer than I ever did anything else in my life. But my heart bled. Tonight would be our last night together.

We had been together many times before she began to talk about her work in the communities. By the time I realised that our relationship formed the very epitome of a conflict of interest I had already come to love her the way a man loves a woman he never sees. If I were to shed tears Joyce DiDonato's voice should have helped me do it. Instead I stared at the ceiling and mouthed along to the foreign words blaring from my portable speaker.

"Piangerò la sorte mia…"

She returned in the evening. Tired from endless meetings. Bubbling with stories she really shouldn't have been telling me. Still we talked and made love. Afterwards, we lay on the bed in silence. I propped myself up on one elbow and looked at her.

I think I have fallen in love with you.

I didn't say it. Her smile was a dagger to my heart. Still I smiled back.

"Hold on," I said, getting up from the bed.

I unlocked the closet safe and looked at the bottle. Old Number 7. When she saw it she sat up with glee.

"You finally opened the bottle!"

"Yes."

"So this is it? No more hotshot businessman travelling the globe?"

"Yes."

"You're really retiring?"

I laughed, "Yes. No more hotshot businessman. Just sunny beaches and tall drinks."

"Wow!"

"I know," I said, and passed her glass, "A toast."

She raised her glass and we drank.

"Where will you go?"

I poured more whiskey.

"Not sure. I've spent a lot of time in hotels in my career, I always wondered what it would be like to own one."

"Here in the South?" she asked hopefully.

I sighed.

When a file landed in your hands from The Shadow you acted and asked questions later. It didn't matter who it was. Our job was to maintain peace in The Union. And Nyararai's influence had grown like a wildfire in the preceding few years. Her ideas had grown beyond simply improving the lives of young children so that they could build a better tomorrow. She had also started educational groups for adults. Women and men were being taught to work together to fight the perceived evils of any one-sided society, patriarchal or otherwise. In remote parts of the lower south, calls had been made for her to run for regional leadership. In some areas, there had even been talk of her becoming The Head of the Union.

And her file had landed on my desk.

She was a threat to peace in The Union. Meetings organised by supporters of her movement ended in violent clashes. Almost on a weekly basis, The Spear had to send officers to calm down the crowds. The Spear's interventions meant anti-riot shields, tear gas and batons. At The Shadow, we were taught from day one that the only way to kill a snake was to strike its head. I knew what happened to men who refused to strike the snake.

"Maybe offshore," I said, watching her as she took a third shot.

She missed the nightstand and the glass fell to the floor.

"Oops," she said, rubbing her eyes and laughing. "Chinhu ichi chino dhaka! Feels like I just drank half of it alone."

A conventional dose of Rohypnol would have taken hours to take effect. The dose I had given was far from conventional. The powerful concoction – prepared by Gwenyambira himself – mixed in with whatever beverage you poured into it and the drinker would be unconscious in minutes. Nyararai flopped onto the bed and I immediately got to work.

Our methods were simple. Malcontents could always be eliminated with ease. I positioned a chair in front of the maidBot in the same position it had been when I was working earlier that day. I put her clothes back on and sat her on the chair. It took several attempts to get her to sit without falling over. Next I opened the maidBot's service panel and placed a screwdriver on her lap. I stepped back and looked at Nyararai. Her breathing was slow. Her eyes fluttered ever so slightly. It would be the last time I ever saw her alive. In the morning, the news would be filled with reports about an explosion at a Union-owned hotel in Gutaguru. A representative of The Spear would report that Nyararai had been the victim of her own botched attempt to sabotage the hotel by maliciously reprogramming a service bot. In the days to follow, more and more evidence would come to light pointing to her terrorist activities, leading to a ban on her organisation.

Once my case was packed, I poured myself one last drink as Amos Mathe. On my way out I flipped the manual switch in the maidBot's service panel. Motors began to turn. Its eyes switched on and began to blink on and off.

Downstairs GM was waiting with a car. I got in. He pushed the start button and stared ahead for a few seconds. Another car's headlights briefly lit up our faces as it drove into the parking area. A group of youths laughed and nodded along to American music inside it.

"At least you won't have to look into her eyes when she goes, wangu," GM said, driving off towards Gutaguru Airport.

I nodded, thinking I was worse off for having looked into them knowing I had chosen safety in The Shadow over her.

INTERLUDE

Bulawayo, Present Day,

The fucking words are stuck in the air between the tip of his pen and the exercise book despite having known for weeks what he wants to say. He has played with the words in his mind, laid foundations, built roads and empires; families and nations. But now he sits in his dimly lit room, staring at the blank page the way a man stares at his wife's lover, wanting to rip it to pieces.

In the next room, the springs of an old bed squeak to the rhythm of the bodies writhing on top of it. The couple do their best to muffle their cries of ecstasy, but the treacherous bed has a story to tell. Titus grabs his overgrown hair and mouths a scream at the ceiling.

It's all *her* fault.

He needs air. He tosses his pen on the book and stands up, stretching. He goes over to the foot of his bed and there he rummages through a pile of dirty clothes for a jacket. Someday soon he will need to attend to the laundry.

He lives in a three bedroomed house in Northern Bulawayo. The bedrooms are occupied by four other tenants. The first is a student from the local university. Dorm fees raise the annual cost of tuition almost double so many students choose to rent instead. The second is a mechanic who never fixes any cars. He always has a lot of money even though he hasn't lifted a spanner in years. The last bedroom belongs to a lecherous old man who shares it with any one of six young girls depending on the state of his finances at the given time. Titus lives in what should be the sitting room. The door that connects it to the rest of the house is locked shut and none of the tenants have ever seen the key. Fortunately for Titus, it means never having to see any of the others unless he needs to use the bathroom.

Her voice haunts him as he opens the outside door.

"Where are you going?"

"I need some air."

"K," she rasps, "bring some for me."

But she is not here.

She is crazy, he thinks as he dispels the reverie with a shake of his head, *but, then again, so am I.*

Through the open door the icy air reaches for him, promising to wrap itself around him and find a home in his bones. He steps outside and shuts the door. The jacket protects his arms and back, but his ears are horribly exposed.

He sighs.

If she was here, the words wouldn't be stuck.

He has never believed in muses. His opinion is that writers use the word to avoid explaining their methods. But it all comes down to pain. And the ability to make art out of it. No muses anywhere. Please and thank you.

But if she was here, the words would not be stuck, and his mind would be focused. His thoughts would not be entangled in nostalgia. Nor the hope that tonight is the night when she bursts through the door like she used to, bearing gifts of take-aways, free booze, and condoms they will never use. She would complain about his work and the hours spent hunched over his desk.

If she was here, he wouldn't miss her.

Two drunk men walk by on the street. One bellows about some referee.

"Uyahlany' uref lwan' umsun'wakhe! Vele yikuthi nxa kudlalwa le Man U, uWebb uyab' ebafeva! Nx!"

The other, whose voice is notably a few octaves higher, laughs and jeers at his companion for being a sore loser. Their arms are draped over each other's shoulders, probably to keep them from falling over. Titus stifles a laugh. The sight reminds him of children singing in the afternoon sun.

Masgonaneeeeeeeeeeeni! Ilanga liyatshisa! Tshisa dokotela!

For a brief, glorious, moment his mind is drawn away from her and he smiles long after the drunkards are gone.

Then his thoughts return to Andile.

His friend dated hers in high school. Inevitably they became a group. Freddy and Khonzile's friends. Titus and Andile gravitated toward each other and after that rumours of them being a couple followed them everywhere. Titus could only wish they were true. She had an eye for someone else. A Kalanga-speaking mutual friend whose full name they could not pronounce so they all called him Amu.

Titus confessed his love for her once. They were drinking at Freddy's house one moonlit Saturday night. She thought he was kidding and laughed it off. He never gathered enough courage to make a second attempt.

"Fuck it."

A tiny cloud escapes his lips as he mutters the words. He can't stand the cold any longer. He turns up the collar of his jacket and re-enters the house. He sits at the desk and spends a few more excruciating minutes trying to write. The effort is wasted. He gets up in anger and switches off the light before getting into bed.

He falls asleep almost immediately, and again she returns to him in his dreams.

AFTERMATH

Harare, 2011

Elias killed the engine and stared straight ahead. They were parked outside The Rainbow Towers. Andile felt as if her heart would hammer all the way up her oesophagus and onto her tongue. She studied her hands. Had they always been this dark? Elias said nothing. The only sound to be heard was their shaky breathing.

She had thoroughly enjoyed the wedding ceremony. To begin with, Elias looked nothing like what she had expected. They were introduced to each other a few weeks prior to the ceremony and to say that Andile was pleasantly surprised would be an understatement. Most of her cousins had been married the same way. The families discussed it and, when the time was right, the child was introduced to her betrothed. For her cousins, said betrothed was often short and overweight, with a belly that could easily be used in those pregnancy adverts in magazines. Just last year her cousin, Nyari, had nearly fainted when they introduced her to Phibion with his overgrown beard and patchy hair. But here was Mr Nyakabe. At 35 he looked nothing like his peers. His belly stayed respectfully behind his belt and he was clean-shaven. His hair was cut in a neat brush cut.

He kept everything light. Throughout the wedding he pointed out his relatives and told funny stories about them. Despite her fear and apprehension, she found herself laughing at his stories and thinking how grateful she was that her husband at least had a healthy sense of humour.

She looked at him again. He was still staring intently at the building ahead of them. He seemed to be in his head too. She wanted to say something. She cleared her throat but no words came out. The sound seemed to bring him back. He opened his door and stepped quickly around the car to open hers. She was afraid she would not be able to stand but her legs surprised her.

"Well," he said, "we're here, Mrs Nyakabe."

She gave him a brief smile and hoped she had succeeded in hiding her fear. She knew that now they were at the hotel her husband would expect to consummate their marriage. It was a recurring topic at the meeting that her mother and aunts held with her the previous day. She could still see her aunt with her zambia tied tight around her waist, gesticulating as if she were trying to dissect the air with her bare hands.

"Umuntu uyavala la, avule la, lala," NaBongi had said, pointing to her mouth, eyes and ears respectively. "Indoda ngubab' ekhaya. Uyangizwa mntakaNobuhle?"

There were eight women there in total, and although Andile couldn't remember all of it, each one had given their input.

"Ngaz' akufic' udinwe njani, engath' ufun' ikhekh' uyaphiwa, uyezwa? Ungathi subalekelwe yindoda lapha subuya kith' uhlihla futhi. Hant' uyab' umncitsha? Pho ufun' ayenzeni?"

"Aklin' endlini futh' umuntu. Ungabi litshapha la. Phel' amadoda law' awayifun' idoti."

"Mhla womtshado vel' ungaqali ukwala lesitho. Ngaphandle nje nxa ufun' ahl' aqale ngok'yading' umakhwapheni. Uyangizwa Andile?"

That last instruction came to her mind as she followed Nyakabe into the hotel. It played itself over and over as they watched the numbers change in the lifts. By the time they got to their room she was almost shaking.

Elias unlocked the door and led her in.

"OK," he said, "why don't you get comfortable while I get the rest of our stuff from the car?"

Andile nodded discreetly and looked around the room. Somewhere far away her mind registered the sound of the door closing as she took everything in, the fresh sheets on the bed, the extra blanket folded at its foot, the kettle and tea mugs on the dresser, and the breath-taking view of Harare through the window. Finally, her legs gave out and she sat down on the bed. She felt a hot tear slide down her face and before she could wipe it away, she was sobbing like a child. Would he be gentle? Would he expect her to participate? To *touch* him?

She had never had a boyfriend. Save for her inexplicable crush on a classmate in high school she had always kept clear of boys because her mother made sure she knew from a young age that girls should not think of love before they were married. Their culture was clear on that. You got married, then you learned the man's habits, how to talk to him, his character, and what he valued. Then, and only then, did you think about love and forever afters.

But none of that had prepared her for this moment. Being in a hotel room with a man who would undoubtedly want to get his money's worth, so to speak. She thought of Nyari again, and the unpleasant story of her first time. She wept bitterly.

She didn't notice that Elias had come back. When he sat down on the bed next to her and put his arms around her she nearly jumped. She let the last of her sobs out. He let her go and took her hand.

"Look, Andile," he said, "I know this isn't easy for you. Being here with a stranger. I'm shitting bricks too! But ang'soze ng'kujahe. I know you're worried about our first night together and it's ok. I don't expect you to do anything you're not comfortable with."

Her eyes were the size of one-dollar coins when she looked at him. She thought she hadn't heard him right. But then she saw the look in his eyes and realised just how nervous he was too. All this time she hadn't realised it, but it was there.

"Asiz'hlalele laph' embhedeni. S'xoxe." He said. "Kumbe s'bukel' iTV."

Andile excused herself and went into the bathroom. Her face was a mess. She washed off what was left of her make-up and looked at her reflection. She was confused. Hadn't NaT said every man expected to 'sample the goods' on the very first night? Was it a trick? She had relaxed a little. But she found she still couldn't loosen up all the way.

She walked back into the room and the English version of Edith Piaf's *No Regrets* was playing from the TV. It was an insurance ad. On the screen was a young man eagerly about to sign a contract with a loan shark. The loan shark was grinning the way Rudd must have grinned when Lobhengula marked the concession with his royal seal. Behind the loan shark stood an oiled-up bouncer in a black vest, also grinning.

Elias chuckled and muttered, "Poor bastard."

She chuckled too. Then she sat on the bed and stared at the TV. Elias handed her the remote.

"See if there's anything you like," he said, "mina leTV saxabana ngo'99."

She couldn't hold back the laugh.

"Laxatshaniswa yini kambe lent' engakhulumiyo?" she asked.

"I spend a lot of my time reading books and watching old documentaries on my laptop," he said, and then shrugged. "Ulamanga futhi. Awuyizwa wena iTV ikhuluma khathesi?"

She laughed again. The evening news had begun.

"So asibone what kind of documentaries you watch."

"Are you sure? Yinto zabo Malcom X laboMandela. Politics."

"Oh," she said, "Ok."

There was a long silence. Andile kept her eyes on the TV. She took a quick glance at him and found he was looking at her. She dropped her eyes. Then turned them back to the TV. Sometime later, she couldn't tell how long, she was about to ask him how long they were going to stay at the hotel when she heard him snore. She turned to him and saw that he had fallen asleep. A wave of relief swept over her. Perhaps he really didn't mean to make her do anything she wasn't ready to do. She unfolded the blanket and gently put it on him. He shifted his weight and got comfortable.

Andile went back around to her side of the bed and sat down. The TV now showed an old black and white Japanese movie with English subtitles. She settled for this and fell asleep a while later. She didn't know it yet, but she was already falling in love with Elias Nyakabe.

Harare, 2017

Titus was in Harare for a writers' workshop when he met Andile again after high school. It was one of those sponsored affairs. Transport and accommodation were covered, and his meal allowance was enough to buy groceries for at least two weeks.

After the second day of the workshop, he walked from the Jameson to an obscure little bar on Julius Nyerere. It was one of those remnants of Rhodesia. Wood panelling all over the bar and chairs that looked like they may have been bought before he was born. Still he thought it was a good enough place to have a beer and people-watch. He got a Black Label and sat down in a corner where he could see everyone. The sounds of Tongai Moyo boomed out of the radio and it seemed to Titus that every song ran longer than ten minutes. The bar hummed with the voices of several conversations.

Titus sipped his beer and took notes.

Three old men were playing dominoes at the table next to his. Between moves they lamented their stolen pensions and reminisced about the good old days. Each sentence ended with a grunt as the speaker slapped his next domino on the table. A gap-toothed gentleman in an ancient flat-cap shouted 'Wash' umsuthu!' as he played his penultimate domino. His rivals had two each.

They both clicked their tongues and the one wearing a black safari hat said, "Watanga, Chitonho!"

Chitonho chuckled and then drank from his glass as the others played their hand. From what Titus could see of the third man's dominoes, he would need a miracle to get back in the game.

"Shit mhani!" the man exclaimed as Chitonho ended the game. He got up and searched his pockets. He found what he was looking for in the breast pocket of his jacket. He pulled out a box of Madison and excused himself. Chitonho and Safari Hat started a new game.

Titus got up too and headed to the men's room. A young man had passed out just inside the toilet. Titus shook his head as he stepped gingerly over him. Had he been here, his father would have pointed out that this was the reason why you should pour water in your beer if you can't handle it. He closed his eyes and hummed to himself as he used the urinal. When he stepped out of the toilet afterward, he froze in his tracks.

She stood at the bar with a whiskey glass in hand. Her black dress clung to her skin as if it had been painted on. She was tall, so her heels made her look like a giant. The afro nearly threw him off, but there was no mistaking her. He composed himself and stepped toward her. He was still going over opening lines in his head when she turned and looked right at him. Her eyes widened in surprise, then her lips curled upwards and she all but leapt into his arms.

"Titus! Oh my god! Wenzani la?" she squealed and then hugged him again.

She was an image of the past. The last echoes of his teenage dreams. Only her face had changed. Various scars stood out on it like checkpoints on a map. She seemed relieved to be seeing a familiar face, but that could have been wishful thinking.

"Ng'yanatha," he said, and grinned. "Besides, I could ask you the same!"

They laughed. He ordered another round for himself and led her to his table. The pensioners seemed to have found somewhere else to be and this was a relief. At least they would have some semblance of privacy. They sipped their drinks and caught up on life during the preceding six years. Who was still in the neighbourhood? Who had children? Who was succeeding in life? She wanted to know everything. Titus filled her in to the best of his abilities. Then he steered the conversation to the question he really wanted to ask. What was she doing in Harare?

"Long story," she said, "but I live here now. Basically, ever since we finished high school."

Titus made a show of checking his watch and replied, "I don't have anywhere important to go."

She chuckled, "I see you still like being dramatic."

"Occupational hazard," he replied, smiling and tapping his notebook with his pen.

She smiled back. But he couldn't help noting how sad her smile was. She looked at her hands then looked back at him.

"Well, I live here with my husband."

He found that even after all this time it drove a knife through his heart. He had always secretly wished he could find her again and that they would ride off into the proverbial sunset together. And here she was confirming his worst fear. That dream would always be just that. He forced another smile.

"Wow! Congratulations! Manj' awus'nxusi?"

"Well it all happened pretty fast. Hant' uyakwaz' ukuthi ng'khaya bangen' ipostori…"

"Oh," he didn't know what else to say. He fumbled for something appropriate to say, then just said, "Yeah… yeah I remember."

They sat in silence for a few minutes. Titus ordered another round. Eventually he had to say something, so he asked the only thing that would come to his mind.

"Manj' umkakh' engak'thol' unatha lami so ebhaw' uzathini?"

She smiled, "Lwana kangen' ebhaw' enje. And even if he did, he's away on business so it's mama's turn to play."

He grinned, "Nhlanhla yami ke! Kumbe vele nguw' obungibiz' ukuthi ngizonathela la instead of the hotel bar."

They laughed again. He savoured the sound of her laughter. Then he told her about his workshop and the little writing he had been doing over the years. Newspaper articles. Some essays for online journals and a blog post or three. He was embarrassed that he still hadn't finished his novel.

"Well," she said, "better finish it before we die, Titus, because neither of us knows when that might happen."

He would have laughed but there was a seriousness about how she said it that unsettled him. He studied her face again and wondered about the scars. He thought her husband might have put them there, but it seemed inappropriate to ask. So instead he commented on her body.

"I must say, maturity is doing you a tonne of favours body wise… or is it true that marriage does that?"

She smiled and said nothing. But there was no mirth in it. He wanted to hug her. He wanted to tell her that everything would be alright. That whatever was wrong would pass. But even in his mind the words sounded limp.

She got up abruptly and said she had to leave. Titus asked her to have one more drink. She said she couldn't. He didn't have a phone, so he asked if she was on Facebook.

"Yeah. Andile Nyakabe."

He said he would say hi sometime and she said that was ok. Then she walked out and left him wondering if they would ever see each other again.

HH 187-19
CRB 29-19

THE STATE
versus
ANDILE MATHE

HIGH COURT OF ZIMBABWE
CHISORO Q
HARARE 22 FEBRUARY 2019

Criminal Trial

Mr J Mudiyayi for the state
Mr C Mbedzi for the accused

CHISORO Q: The accused was an adult female aged 28 years. The deceased was the accused's husband. The parties had been married for 8 years. It is alleged that on the 16th of February 2018 at their marital home at number 3 Garden Lane in Avondale, the accused did wrongfully and unlawfully murder the deceased Elias Nyakabe, who was an adult male aged 43, by stabbing him with a knife and thus inflicting certain fatal injuries. The accused offered a plea of not guilty to the charge and raised the defence of self-defence.

The material facts without regurgitating them can be summarised as follows:

1. The deceased and the accused were married through an arranged traditional marriage in 2011.
2. The marriage was not a happy one. The deceased was abusive toward the accused and would often beat her. The accused reported several such matters at Avondale Police station but would then later withdraw the charges after seemingly reconciling with the deceased. The deceased was also in the habit of bringing women home and having sexual intercourse

with them in full view of the accused.

3. The deceased is alleged to have come home drunk at around 21:00 hrs and begun insulting his wife and accusing her of being a prostitute. The accused denied the accusations and instead raised the issue of the deceased bringing women home frequently.
4. This angered the deceased and the issue escalated into a heated verbal exchange. Eventually the deceased began to assault the accused with his hands indiscriminately all over her body
5. The accused, in reacting to the assault, ran into the kitchen and armed herself with a kitchen knife. This knife was produced as exhibit 3. It was smeared with blood and it had a straight blade. It is not disputable that the knife was used to inflict wounds of such severity and magnitude as shall be described later.
6. The deceased persisted with the assault even though the accused had armed herself with the knife.
7. The accused reacted by randomly attacking the deceased with the knife. The cuts and injuries inflicted by this attack are detailed in the post-mortem report submitted as exhibit 2. The photographs taken show that the injuries inflicted on the body of the deceased are gruesome, that is to say they are unpleasant to look at. The floor around the body of the deceased was covered in blood.
8. The deceased eventually succumbed to his injuries and the accused left the house and made a report of the incident at Avondale Police Station. Officers present at the station have stated that she was covered in blood, but they recognised her because of previous domestic violence related incidents.
9. The officers quickly ran to the house with the aim of assisting but upon arrival they found the deceased already dead.

Doctor H Jinabhai subsequently conducted a post-mortem examination on 20 February 2018 and compiled his report. He identified the cause of death as post haemorrhagic shock. The following are some highlights of the report:

i. The deceased's clothing was blood soaked.

ii. The body had stabs and cuts consistent with sharp force injuries.

iii. The body of the deceased did not have any evidence of resuscitation attempts, thereby agreeing with accused's statements that she took no further action on the deceased after seeing that he was losing his strength.

iv. An examination of the head, face and neck showed no evidence of injury due to blunt force trauma. There was however a superficial cut running vertically along his left trapezius muscle. This cut was 3.5cm in length but was not severe.

v. The right side of the neck had an obliquely running stab-cut wound with a squared off shape where it began and a pointed corner where it ended. It measured 3.8cm and gaped by 2cm at the centre. This wound was so severe that the carotid artery was cut.

vi. The upper left arm had a deep incisional wound that measured 2.3cm and gaped by 0.7cm at the centre.

The doctor highlighted that there was 1 stab wound and 2 incisional wounds on the body. The nature of the injuries was grievous and fatal, which led to the deceased losing blood amounting to at least 1/3 of the blood (which is about 2 litres). Such high volumes of blood loss cause circulatory failure and precipitate death in minutes or even seconds. Dr Jinabhai highlighted the cause of death as being haemorrhages and shock.

In order to ascertain the sustainability of the accused's defence of self-defence, the court must 'take due account of the circumstances in which the accused found himself/herself including any knowledge or capability he or she may have had and any stress or fear that may have been operating in all the circumstances.'[1] It is with this in mind that the court must proceed to analyse the evidence presented by the state and the defence.

The state case was built on the evidence of constables Milton Mwenje and Shaurai Makonese, and Doctor Hittesh Jinabhai. The defence case was limited to the *viva voce* evidence by the accused.

The constables were present at Avondale Police Station when the accused presented herself on the night in question. They were the ones to discover the body of the deceased upon initial investigation. They also corroborated the statements of the accused wherein she said she was constantly abused by her husband. Constable Makonese went on to say that when they saw her on that night, she appeared to have been beaten up in the manner they had become accustomed to, but what shocked them was the amount of blood on her clothes.

Doctor Jinabhai's evidence was the post-mortem report, which indicates that the deceased lost approximately 2 litres of blood and such amount of blood loss accelerates death. The injuries are consistent with the accused's statement that she attacked the deceased indiscriminately in her efforts to defend herself. The nature of the injuries does in fact reveal that they were inflicted randomly with mild to severe force. While death was not intended or foreseen as a possible outcome by the accused, it remains that she acted with negligence of the highest degree in her conduct and failed to guard against any possible loss of life. She stabbed the deceased in the neck, and this led to the death of the deceased. The choice of the accused to use an inherently dangerous weapon was clearly a negligent one. The defence did not present any evidence to show that this was indeed the only line of defence available to the accused. They failed to show that the accused could not have avoided this assault on the deceased by proceeding to any other area besides the kitchen. In this case, a knife became the chosen weapon of defence.

The state argued that a custodial sentence was appropriate. The deceased evidently sustained serious injuries. The accused acted negligently in using a sharp knife to defend herself. The courts have stated and restated that domestic disputes should be resolved amicably, and that violence must not be seen as a resolution to such disputes. The court was urged to ensure that the punishment fit the crime.

Counsel for the accused, Mr C Mbedzi, argued for leniency in the court's approach to this matter. He urged the court to consider that the incident occurred last year and the accused has been in remand prison ever since. She did not waste the court's time putting up false defences which would have necessitated a full trial. She expressed deep sorrow and regret for what happened. The accused is 28 years old and has suffered greatly at the hands of the deceased. The court was urged to take into consideration that had it not been for the malicious behaviour of the deceased towards the accused during the course of their marriage, she might not even be standing in the dock. He raised an intriguing argument arising from an old case in the English courts. I have had the opportunity to review the case cited by the defence.

In R v Ahluwalia [1992] ALL ER 889 it was held (per headnote) as follows:-

> "The appellant, Ahluwalia, suffered abuse and violence from her husband for years. After one violent evening, she went to bed thinking about her husband's behaviour and could not sleep. She finally went downstairs poured petrol into a bucket, lit a candle, went to her husband's bedroom and set it on fire. Her husband died from these injuries. Ahluwalia pleaded manslaughter on grounds that she did not intend to kill him, only to inflict pain. She also pleaded the defence of provocation on grounds of her treatment during the marriage. Ahluwalia was convicted of murder and appealed the decision.

> At the time of the trial there was a medical report showing that at the time of the killing, the defendant was suffering from endogenous depression. It was overlooked and the appellant was not consulted as to the possibility of investigating it further. The appeal was therefore allowed and a re-trial was ordered."

The defence of self-defence is not available to the accused in this issue. She chose to defend herself using a sharp knife and thus acted negligently in causing the death of her spouse. The rate at which the court deals with domestic violence cases is deplorable. It is, however, the court's position that killing cannot be condoned even under such circumstances. Regarding the case referenced by the defence counsel, I find that the cases are dissimilar. There has been no evidence tendered to the court to show that the accused was in fact suffering from any form of depression. The material facts of the case, and the details of the events leading up to the death of the deceased are now known only to the accused.

What I do accept is that she is an abused woman, and while the court considers this a huge factor in determining a sentence it must be stated emphatically that it frowns upon the use of violence in resolving domestic disputes. While having failed to produce any evidence of the cause of the fight besides what the accused has told us, there are several issues that the court cannot ignore:

i. That the accused immediately went to the police station upon realising that the deceased was incapacitated
ii. That the accused did not try to conceal the crime or tamper with evidence
iii. That the accused, while invoking the defence of self-defence, acted negligently in choosing to arm herself with a sharp knife.
iv. That she was regularly abused by the deceased.
v. That the accused was, in fact, badly beaten up on the night of the incident and had several injuries

vi. That the accused, while having acted negligently, did not set out to kill the deceased but acted merely in the heat of the moment.

It is the court's position, that citizens must resolve all disputes peacefully. While the court may not close its eyes to the background of domestic violence in this matter, it is imperative that we uphold and preserve the sanctity of human life. It is not a matter of dispute that the conduct of the deceased triggered the reaction from the accused. However, it was the accused's responsibility to act with consideration of the consequences of her actions. She behaved negligently and brought about the death of the deceased. The court does take into consideration that the accused did not attempt to hide her actions and immediately sought assistance at the nearest police station. The accused has also shown contrition for her actions, having been seen shaking her head and weeping throughout the greater part of these proceedings.

For the court to return a verdict of murder with actual intent, the court must be satisfied beyond any doubt that either the accused desired to bring about the death of the victim or reasonably foresaw that as a result of her conduct death was a substantial possibility. In this case, the accused was in an emotional state. It has been argued that her actions were driven by 'abused woman syndrome' as reflected in the argument from the defence. However, there has been no evidence to support this claim. The accused has not offered a defence of provocation and her plea for the defence of self-defence cannot be admitted. She armed herself with a knife and this inherently increased the risk of injury and, as is unfortunately evident in this case, death.

In the result, and accordingly, we do not believe that the accused set out to murder the deceased. She is, therefore, acquitted on the charge of murder and found guilty with respect to culpable homicide.

Hardly a day passes without the courts dealing with cases of domestic violence. It is appalling that an individual can perpetuate such ferocious violence towards one whom he has promised lifelong love. That so many do and get away with it is an indictment to our laws and domestic practices. The message from the courts is that violence cannot be tolerated as a means of resolving disputes. It has no place within a modern society.

In the circumstances, I do hereby sentènce the accused thus:
8 years imprisonment of which 2 years are suspended for 5 years on condition that the accused shall not within that period commit any offence involving the loss of human life as defined in ss 47 or 49 of the Code[2]. The sentence includes time served.

Effective sentence (five) 5 years imprisonment.

National Prosecuting Authority's Office, the state's legal practitioners
Messrs C Mbedzi and Associates, the accused's legal practitioners

[1] Criminal Law(Codification and Reform) Act [Chapter 9:23] (the Code)
[2] Criminal Law(Codification and Reform) Act

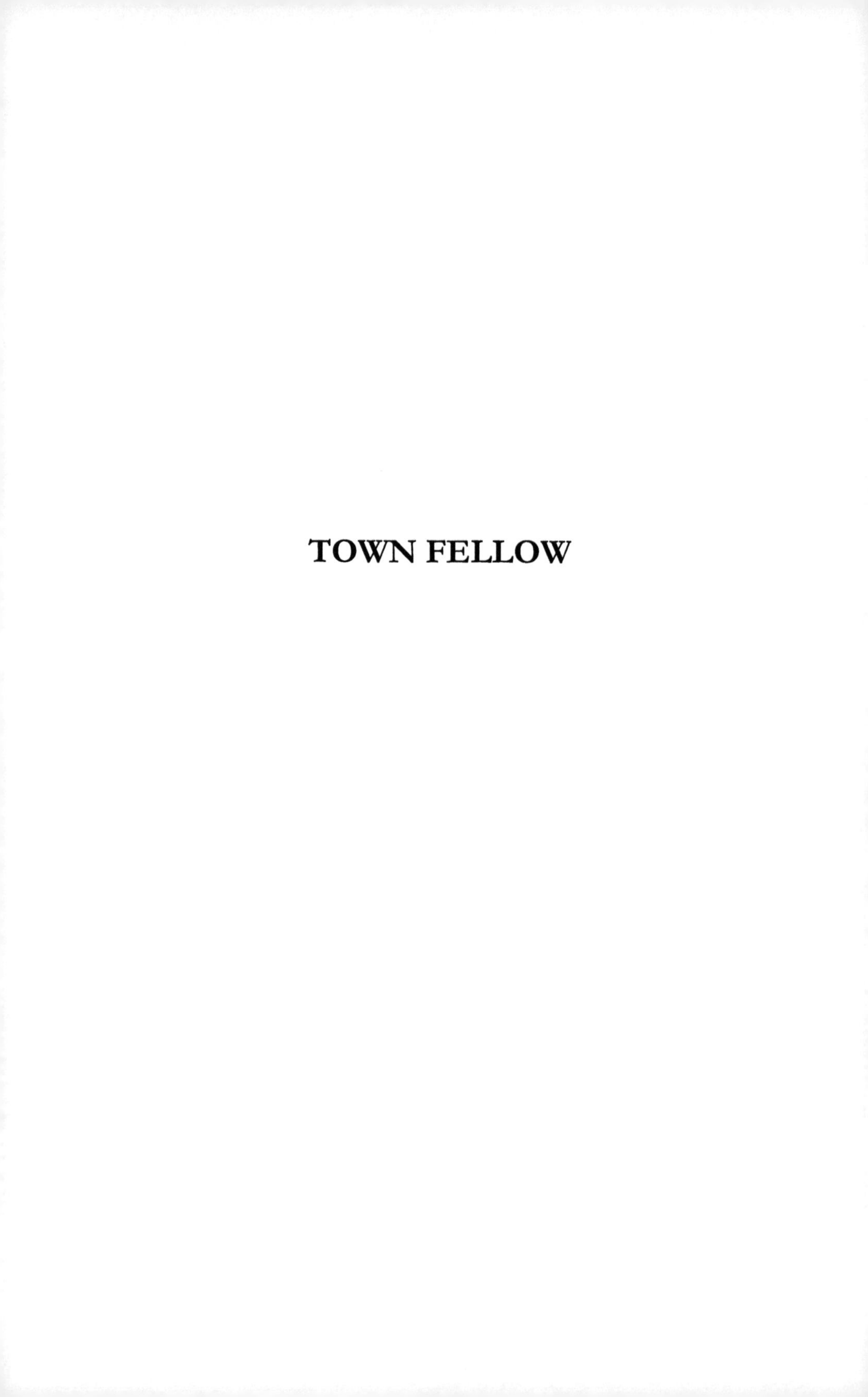

TOWN FELLOW

We have to shout to hear each other. Tawaz is talking in that way that he usually does. Like we are his boys and he is the boss. I don't blame him. Minus a round or two he is paying for everyone's beers. He always pays for everyone's beers.

Right now he is talking about living in South Africa. We've all been talking about rising prices and the conversation crept to how much food costs in other countries. His hands are held up like he's holding an enormous burger.

"Boys inini I used to eat kuSout," he bellows, "kwakulamachips so aweChicken Licken ayebuya le2 litres yeCoke."

He laughs that way people laugh when they are enjoying the memory as much as they are enjoying telling the story.

"Ayemaneng' amachips lawana, okokuthi wawungek' uwaqede wedwa. But mina ngaseng'waqeda!"

Gilbert and Munya laugh.

I smile and say, "Ya that sounds like a lot of chips, bra."

"Ndoda!" he says.

He always says that when he agrees with you.

The waitress appears with another round of beers. Carling Black Label for me, Zambezis for Munya and Gilbert, and a Castle Lite for Tawaz. Tawaz grabs the waitress's butt and whispers something in her ear. She giggles and playfully pushes him away.

"Aah iwe Tawanda kwana mhani!"

I wonder if there's anyone in the city who doesn't know Tawaz. Seems like every bar we go to he's greeting waitresses and other patrons. Most of them know him by name. We never leave a bar without some random person stopping him to talk or without a waitress making eyes at him.

"Must be nice," I mutter.

"What?" Gilbert shouts.

"Nothing. Just thinking out loud."

He bursts into laughter, "You shouldn't talk to yourself so much,

Bukowski."

I cringe. He's been calling me that ever since he heard I write poetry. It's annoying. Bukowski is the only poet he knows so he uses his name to make fun of me. I want to say something mean about him. Maybe say something about how small minds always find joy in belittling those who have chosen not to live in ignorance's shadow. But he is twice my size, and I'm not looking for a fight today. I grin and sip my beer.

Safari bar is busier than usual. There seems to be a much younger crowd but I can see some of the old veterans laughing and talking loud. There's an old schoolteacher of mine talking to a girl who looks like she was reading *Sunrise Readers* when I wrote my A-levels. I've also spotted an older guy I sometimes talk to when I come here alone.

When my mind returns to the conversation Gilbert and Munya are talking about leaving. They have a work event tonight. Tawaz suggests we down our beers and find somewhere else to go.

"Bottoms up," he says.

I gulp the rest of my beer and when I finish, he is looking me with a huge smile on his lips.

"Bra, are you that thirsty?" There is laughter beneath his voice.

I chuckle. He lifts his own beer and when he is done we go outside. He needs to smoke, so I stand with him while he fumbles through his pockets for a Madison.

"Excuse me, boss," his phone shouts suddenly, "you have a text message."

He pulls out the phone and reads the text, then his face lights up. He makes a phone call.

"Jones! Wuyai kuSafari ka!"

He listens.

"Ah horaiti mira tiuye ikoko. But hell yeah I'm in!"

He hangs up and grins.

"So Jones is in need of a couple of wingmen," he says, "apparently he invited Khanyisa for drinks and she brought two friends along."

I grin, "Sounds like a party! I wanted to see Rudo today but she's with her boyfriend anyway."

Tawaz laughs, "This friends-with-benefits thing is gonna get you killed one of these days."

We get into the car and drive off.

"So Jones is still seeing Khanyisa?" I ask, "Nice!"

"Haa bra would you leave those boobs?" Tawaz says and then grins.

"Touché."

We turn onto JMN Nkomo Street and head towards Unity Village. There are some girls in shorts taking pictures below the brazen Nkomo. It looks pretty awesome when the lights are on.

When we get to Unity Village we find Tawaz parked in the centre-parking. Khanyisa's boobs are in the front seat. She's eating chips. There are two other girls in the back seat. My eyes are drawn to the one behind the driver's seat. Dark girls are my kryptonite. She also has a pout which seems suggestive to me. Jones jumps out of the car beaming.

"Tawaz! Morris! Zvirisei guys?"

"Ndeip ndeip?" Tawaz shouts back.

"Mike Jones! Long time, bra. Usharp?" I say, slapping his palm.

"Yeah yeah!" he says grabbing my hand and giving me half a hug with his free arm. "Tirikuita sei, boys?"

"Ah tiudze plan yako sha!" Tawaz says, "Isn't you're the one who invited us?"

Jones laughs and asks, "Did you see who's in the back seat?"

Tawaz looks and smiles.

"Karys! Saka you're just gonna sit there as if awus' kundiona?" he says to the rear window.

Karys gets out of the car smiling, "Ko iwe wanga usingadi kundimhoresa here?"

They both laugh and he hugs her. I'm thinking this is great because she's too tall and too light for me anyway. Jones looks at me and slightly jerks his head towards his car. I grin and nod.

"So what is the plan, bra?" I ask.

"We wanted to go braai some meat but kwete kuHartsfield. Too many people. So we're still thinking about where to go."

"What about Redwood?" Khanyisa asks through the window.

Everyone agrees Redwood would be awesome. Karys volunteers to ride with Tawaz and I climb into the back seat of Jones's car with the other friend.

She smiles at me and hands me a quarter full bottle of Famous Grouse.

"You're rather late to the party," she says.

"A poet is never late," I say, "He arrives precisely when he means to."

She laughs and then responds, "You stole that from Gandalf."

"I like you already," I tell her before I take a sip from the bottle.

The Grouse rolls smoothly over my tongue and into my throat. I look at the bottle and then back at her.

"Damn, girl! You drank all this by yourself?"

"I had help from Jones and Karys. But Karys is gone and Jones has switched to light beer now." She rolls her eyes as she says 'light beer.'

"Jones shame on you! Don't you know drinking light beer…"

He interjects, "Yeah yeah we've all heard it before, bra. Leave me alone."

I chuckle.

She asks, "What were you going to say?"

"That drinking light beer is like going down on your sister. It'll probably taste the same but that shit is just wrong!"

She bursts into laughter. It's a boisterous laugh. The likes of which I've never heard coming from a girl before. When she recovers she shakes her head and says, "You're gross."

"It's the truth though."

We're on Plumtree Road now. It's too dark to see much besides the lights in the distance. Is that Nketa or Mganwini? I can't be sure. She's looking out of her window. Nothing to see on that side except milestones and trees.

"So clearly these guys aren't going to introduce us," I say, "my name is Morris. And I want to call you something other than 'she' in my head."

"Nyasha," she says.

"Well it's my very good honour to meet you, Nyasha."

"Feeling is mutual Morris Minor."

I can't help but laugh, "I must say I never thought there was much to do with my name. How do you even know that car?"

"I know a lot of things."

"Cool."

There's a silence between us after that. I have to say something. Anything. So I say what's been on my mind since we first saw her in the car.

"I can't help staring at your lips, Nyasha."

She turns towards me with a smile on her face. I can't quite decipher it, but for a second I think she already knows what I want to say and I brace myself for a putdown.

"Oh really? And why is that?" she asks. Then she licks them. Not like my-lips-are-dry licking either, but sexy, get-over-here licking. She takes her time too.

"Well, for starters, I'm wondering how good a kisser you are."

She doesn't say anything at first. I'm reminded of a time in form one when I had this huge crush on the girl from the house opposite my home. Her name was Buhle. And she lived up to her name. One time my friends JC and Tate arranged a meeting for us. I told her I wanted her and she said she didn't want me. I'm waiting now for that same crushed feeling, in the back seat of Jones' car.

But she surprises me.

"Well, there's only one way to find out, isn't there?"

I can't believe what I'm hearing. Then she moves to the centre of the seat and closes her eyes. She puckers up. I'm thinking it's a joke so I lean in too.

We kiss. I don't know for how long. Her lips are soft but firm. She slips her tongue through my lips and explores my mouth. Our tongues dance in my mouth and in hers. My mind is racing though. I mean damn, that was fucking easy! We kiss.

She only stops me when my hand reaches the moist warmth between her thighs.

"We didn't say anything about those lips," she says.

"Well, besokumnandi so I couldn't help myself."

"Well, the night is still young so relax."

She drops me a wink. I smile and look out the window.

When we get to Redwood it's deserted. The only person there is a security guard who tells us that they were closed today. Nyasha and the other girls go for a bathroom break and I stand with Tawaz and Jones while they smoke. Jones is the first to speak.

"Dude! What in the fuck just happened?"

"Lam' ang'kwazi," I respond, "I imagined that conversation going any one of a thousand ways and that wasn't really one of them."

"Bra!" he exclaims, "All I heard was 'are you a good kisser' and then it was mncwa mncwa the whole way!"

"Haha you lie!" says Tawaz.

Jones keeps talking, "Dude, even Khanyisa stopped talking. We were just looking at the road thinking these people are about to fuck right there!"

"Bra, even I don't know what happened. One minute I was tasting Famous Grouse and the next I was tasting Nyasha."

Tawaz says, "Ah that's heavy game."

"Man, if I had known I had this much power!" I say.

We all laugh.

The girls return and we all agree to go to BAC. It's almost ten now so we might as well go to the club. Nyasha and I sit together again. We chat all the way back. Turns out she's 20 and in her second year at NUST. Computer Science. She asks what I do. I tell her I drink beer and write poetry. She playfully punches my arm and tells me to be serious. I grin and say I am being serious.

But there is no kissing on the return trip.

There are lots of people at the BAC parking lot. As we drive in we see a topless man dancing and singing along (with his own version of the lyrics) to A$ap Rocky's *Fuckin' Problems*. We all laugh because it looks more like he's having a seizure. We find a free spot next to a green Toyota Corolla with tinted windows. The driver's window is open just a crack and there's thick grey smoke coming out of it.

After we get our stamps Tawaz gets me a round of Black Label and tells me to shout when I'm empty. Then he disappears off to the dance floor. The girls have all gone to the bathroom. I find a free table and lean on it. The numerous TVs in the bar show a repeat of an English Premier League match. The sound is off but I still enjoy watching the pictures. The DJ plays some dance hall song I've never heard before. I nod along and eavesdrop on a group of girls behind me talking about the men they came with. It's hilarious. Nyasha and the others are probably somewhere doing the same thing.

A pair of tiny cold hands blocks my vision. Their owner says, "Guess who?"

"Angela Basset."

She laughs. "No, guess again."

"If I get it right do I get another kiss?"

Nyasha lets me go and comes around to stand in front of me.

"Nice try, Mr!" she says.

Then she starts to dance. This girl can move. I stand there for a minute wondering what to do. I'm a terrible dancer, but I decide this moment is worth more than my ego. I stand behind her and try to keep up with her hip movements. It's a clumsy affair but eventually we find our rhythm and I actually enjoy myself. She keeps looking back at me and smiling like she's having the time of her life. Eventually she stops dancing and grabs my hand.

"Let's go cool off outside."

I follow her to the parking lot. There are people everywhere. Some smoking, others just standing and talking. I see my brother's friend Charmaine and she waves at me. Nyasha leads me to Jones' Car. All the doors are locked so we just stand there and lean on the car.

"Well," I say, "I'd say the night is pretty mature now. And here we are all alone."

"Yes we are."

She looks into my eyes like she knows what I'm thinking and then takes a sip of her cider. When she pulls the bottle away from her mouth I lean in. She closes her eyes and I stop a few centimetres short of her face. She leans in the rest of the way and our lips lock. I can feel things lighting up in me. There's a tingling at my waist and in the spaces between my toes. She puts her arms around my neck and holds my head. I pull her in closer. The world ceases to exist.

We stop to catch our breath and she looks at me with dilated pupils and the ghost of a smile on her lips.

"So," she asks, "am I a good kisser?"

"I really think you should charge for this."

We laugh. Then Khanyisa speaks up from somewhere behind me.

"So vele lin' alitshiywa lodwa?"

I laugh. Nyasha doesn't say anything. Jones suggests that maybe they should follow our lead and I laugh again. Turns out we're moving. Karys and Khanyisa aren't feeling the vibe here so we're going someplace else. Karys suggests The Lounge.

Jones shrugs and says, "Why not?"

When we get to The Lounge there is a queue as long as the original snake. The usual crowd of people try to negotiate their way in without joining the Queue. Tawaz tells us to join the queue – just in case – while he talks to the bouncer. Nyasha puts her arms around me and leans her head on my chest. Jones raises an eyebrow and I raise both of mine twice.

Next thing we see four guys dragging Tawaz away from the door. They are shouting at him and he is shouting back. Two of them have him by the collar. Jones and I don't even signal. We're there in a matter of seconds.

"Ah ah madoda!" I shout, "Alilanhloni, lifun' ukulwa lomunt' oyedwa lina liyifour?"

"Voetsek wena. Mind your own business," one of them says. He has a gold tooth but the rest of him doesn't look like he can afford a gold tooth.

"Yikho kany' engikwenzayo, my guy," I retort.

Next thing we're all shouting at each other and I grab one of the guys holding Tawaz and pull him away. He's wearing this ugly old blue summer shirt with a picture of a vintage car on it. He turns around and slaps me. I stop thinking right there. My fist connects with his jaw almost at the same time as I launch the other one. He utters a yelp. The others all turn on me. Tawaz and Jones start swinging randomly as well. Nyasha and the rest of the girls are somewhere behind us shouting at us to stop but it's too late. This whole thing has turned into a full-on brawl.

A sharp pain bursts into my left flank and explodes across my belly. We're outnumbered, and the free man in the other group has just cut me with an old pocketknife. I fall to my knees. My abdomen feels like it's on fire. I can hear women screaming. I'm falling sideways now. I can see the ground coming up towards me but I can't stop it. The last thing I see is Tawaz rushing toward me and the other guys running away.

And then there is nothing but darkness.

*

When I open my eyes again I'm standing in the doorway of an old bar. The walls are littered with rock paintings. But instead of hunter-gatherers these paintings show men and women in positions of drunkenness and immorality. Some of the figures are playing instruments. I can see a guitar, a djembe, trumpet, even a saxophone. I step forward and notice a couple of portraits just after the entryway. The first is a beautiful young woman. She is bare-chested and feeding an infant. The other is an old jazz-musician. I can't remember his full name, but I think his first name is Carter. He is sweating and singing into a black mic and the painting is captioned "Looking for a fox…"

I walk towards the counter and when I get there, I look at one of the seats before sitting down. It's made from a tree stump. It has too many rings to count. There aren't a lot of people in the bar. The barman shows up from a back room. I can't see his face. It almost looks like it has been blurred out the way they do on the news when they want to hide someone's identity. I ask him for a Black Label and he points to a sign behind the bar.

It reads: Whiskee or Milke

I ask for the 'whiskee' and wonder why anyone would order 'milke' at a bar.

I freeze with the whiskey glass almost touching my lips. In the mirror behind the bar I can see my cousin Themba coming up to me. He moved to South Africa in 2013 to look for work like everyone else. Rumour has it he joined a notorious gang of crooks and wasted no time in establishing his own infamy. We buried him last year after he was gunned down in a botched bottle-store heist. But here he is, grinning at me and sitting down next to me. He greets me with the same old nickname he had for me when I visited his family in Zimnyama as a child.

"Town Fellow! Zkhuphani?"

I don't say anything. My eyes roll towards him, then my head follows, and my mouth hangs open.

"Relax mafana. I know how weird this is. But it's me. I'm dead but it's me."

I close my mouth and swallow hard. His knowledge of the fact that he is dead brings no comfort.

"So bakuhlinzile mfana?"

"How…" I stop and clear my throat. "How do you know that?"

The barkeeper brings him a glass of milk. Themba picks it up and gestures toward my tummy. I look down. My guts are hanging out of belly and my trousers are soaked in blood. My mouth opens wide.

"Don't scream," he says. "I've seen some terrible things happen whenever a new arrival screams here."

"Where is here?" I ask.

"I don't exactly know," he tells me, then he takes another sip of milk and continues, "All I know is I've seen all this before. You're sitting there with your guts in your lap and you couldn't feel a thing."

He pulls up his shirt and reveals several scars dotted on his chest.

"When I got here kwakufiwa ngobuhlungu. But I was here barely three minutes and then it started to heal. By the time ngizohlala laph' ohlezi khona the pain and the wounds were completely gone."

"Kungaphi lapha, T-man?" I ask again.

"Kusebhawa, mzala," he says, the way you would explain maths to a child. "Ukuthi ngeyangaphi angazi. But kusebhawa."

"So abantu bengafa babuya la?"

"Angitshongo njalo," says Themba, before calmly taking another sip of milk, "Mina ngafikela la. Ngahlala la. Abanye bayafika baphinde bahambe. NjengoAunty."

"Umasalu?"

"Wen' ungazi ngilawuph' omuny' uAunty?" He doesn't wait for a response, "I don't know how long I have been here. But uAunty laye wake wafika kudala. Saxoxa, just like how you and I are talking now. Yasikhal' ifoni leyana. Wasehamba."

He points to a red rotary phone behind the bar. I shake my head at this impossible dream. I was in a fight. I got stabbed. This must be a dream. I'm probably on my way to the hospital as we speak. Themba bursts into laughter.

"Town Fellow, akula phupho lapha. Sesingatshona s'phikisana kodwa njengoba ng'tshilo usebhawa la. Uyedlula. Mina owam' umsebenzi ngowokukulibazisa nje ifon' ingakakhali."

"How is this even possible?" I mutter.

"Asazi, ndoda," Themba says, "But I've seen a few of you travellers over the years."

I stare at him.

He shrugs and finishes off the rest of his milk.

"Ifon' yakho sizangena manje, mzala. Bazakuph' ama instructions."

He looks at my glass and then points, "You better drink that."

I down the whiskey. He looks at me for a while then asks about his father.

"Haven't seen him in a while, T-man," I say. "I haven't seen anyone in a while."

He nods and says, "Yeah, sure. Life and all that."

The rotary phone rings. Themba smiles and looks at me. The barkeeper answers then he picks up the phone and comes towards me. He hands me the receiver. The lady on the other side of the line does not waste any time.

She speaks in an official monotone, "Mr Moyo, uzabuyela ngakini kungekudala. Endleleni lapha uzaboniswa okunye okuqondane lawe. Ukukhumbule konke ozakubona ungavuka ngoba kuqakathekile. Nxa ungabeka phansi ucingo ngicela uqonde emnyango. Ngiyabonga."

There is a loud click and then the line goes quiet. I turn to say something to Themba but he is gone already. In fact the bar is deserted now. I stand up and walk towards the door. The handle is warm. I pull it down and open the door. A bright white light fills the frame as I open it. I can hear singing, but only just. Sounds like a choir singing *Ngiyamthanda Umsindisi*, but I can't be sure.

I step into the light.

*

TOWN FELLOW

Kulolimi esasilukhuluma kudala. Angisalwazi khathesi kodwa ngisalukhumbula mbijana. Lwalusinda ulimi. Lungihlekisa ngabantu nxa ngikhuluma isindebele, kakhulu ngingathi 'gogo.' Babekholisa kakhulu. Kodwa khathesi sengizazela sona isindebele nje.

Namhla bekulusuku lwami lokuqala es'kolo. Izolo ntambama umama ungifundise is'khiwa. Ungifundise u'Hello!' lo'How are you?' Ngifike ngabuza uMiss wangipha i*smile* esikhulu.

Nges'khathi setiye kulomfanyana ebesidlala laye. Angazi ukuthi kusuke kwathini kodwa ungitshaye amakhala nge'sbhakera. Angikaze ngilibone igazi elinengi soya. Bekungani kuvulwe impompi lapha emakhaleni ami. Yena lokuthi ungitshayeleni angazi. Ubuso bakhe besobubomvu njani! Siqale sidlala kuhle nje. Besilezimota. Omunye lomunye edrayiva eyakhe. Sithe sesisiyazibeka uMiss esethe iskhathi setiye sesiphelile nangu umfana evuka ubhova. Watshintsha ubuso bababomvu gebhu. Wangidutshuza emakhaleni. Ngikhale iskhathi eside uMiss engigezisa etoilet.

Ngabe bengisazi iskhiwa njengaye umfana lwana ngabe ngiyakwazi ukuthi ngitshayelweni.

*

I've been here before.

I'm walking down the street with Buhle from the house opposite ours. She's in a short grey dress with horizontal stripes around it. Her hair is cut. She smells like Geisha and Malizia. We're on the second leg of our walk around the neighbourhood. JC and Tate told her that I have something to say to her. She keeps asking what it is, and I keep changing the subject. I want to tell her that I can't stop thinking about her. That she is on my mind when I go to bed at night and in the morning when I wake up. I want to tell her that it's her I'm thinking of every time Shaggy's *Angel* plays on *Coke on the Beat*. But my mouth dries up. My tongue feels too thick and my heart tries to break through my ribcage.

I have been here before.

This happened years ago. Buhle and I are adults now. My mind races. Am I being given a second chance? Maybe this time I can tell her how I really feel!

I'm still thinking about this when she stops at the intersection that connects my house to Mountain View Shopping centre.

"Uthe ufun' ukung'tshela something. Kuyini?" she asks.

It has to be different this time. A second chance! I open my mouth to tell her how I feel, hoping to dazzle her since now I'm more in control of language and words. Instead the same old lame line drops out of my mouth.

"Ng'the ngiyakufuna."

She responds almost immediately, "Manje mina ng'the ang'kufuni."

My heart sinks to my feet. I can't think of anything else to say after that. I stare at the ground. When I look up she is already halfway up the block. She meets JC and Tate. She tells them something and they both burst into laughter.

I don't want to live out the rest of this cruel afternoon. Not again.

Thankfully light fills the world.

*

I can't see anything. There is too much light. I can hear pumps and people talking. I can't move either. I try to say something but my lips won't budge. Someone is praying loudly nearby. I lie still and listen. They are praying in English but the words don't make sense to me.

*

The light fades.

My eyes are closed. When I open them I'm sitting at Cafe Baku with Tate and JC. JC has the locks he cut off after we finished first year at University. I want to ask him what's going on but I can't. There's a bottle of Black Label beer on the table in front of me. The room is spinning. I'm trying to keep track of the conversation at the table but I can't. Recognition begins to force its way to the front of my mind. I remember this day. Earlier we poured a bottle of Breakers into a bucket of Ingwebu and we all shared it. JC, Tate, myself, and some friends of Tate's from school. That was at Manor Hotel. On the way here, to Baku, I waved at a whore at Manor. She asked me if I had money to pay for what I was looking for. I told her I wasn't looking for her. She spat in my direction.

Tate pokes me in the side and I open my eyes. A newcomer has joined us.

"NguSmindlo jeki lo. Ng'geleza laye," Tate says to me. He turns to Smindlo and says, "Lo yibest friend yam' uMorris."

Did Tate just call me his best friend!? I didn't know that until today. I mumble a greeting and try to be cool. I had too much to drink. It was my first time and I had too much to drink. I stand up abruptly. The bathroom seems miles away, but I get there eventually and rush into the only empty stall I can find. All the Ingwebu comes pouring out. I don't know how long I kneel before the porcelain throne. Eventually I pass out on the floor.

When I wake up again one of Tate's friends from school is going through my pockets. I try to grab his hands but I'm too weak. It feels like my hands weigh a tonne. He pulls out the only money I have and counts it with a grin on his face. Three brown bearer cheques. Sixty thousand dollars.

I mutter an insult about his mother and tell him I'm going to get him. He kicks me in the stomach and stuffs my notes in his pocket before walking out.

I'm almost on my feet when JC walks in. I don't know how much time has passed but he is here looking for me anyway. He catches me as I'm about to fall again.

"Aah Morris jeki wena sok'mel' uyelala ngoba lapha sokuy'lahla," he says, walking me towards the door.

"Ngisharp mina," I drawl.

He laughs at me and shakes his head. I look at him and try to smile. When we step into the bar again everyone stares. Tate sees us and takes up my other side quickly. We step towards the door. Tate says something but I don't hear.

We walk into the light and it consumes everything.

*

There is only darkness. I feel cold. I can hear people talking but they are too far away. I try to call out for help but my mouth doesn't make a sound. I try to stand but I can't move.

A tear rolls down the side of my face.

*

I remember this day. It's New Year's Day of 2009. I spent it at Mama's stall at the shops. There are jars full of sweets and other treats in the vegetable rack in front of me. We also sell tomatoes, onions and chomolia.

There's a beautiful woman standing in front of me. The guy she's with seems wrong for her. But they're having a good time. They bought a packet of Charhons Vanilla Creams and now they're sharing it. He's telling lots of jokes and every time she laughs I feel a stab of jealousy. I wish I could get a girl to laugh like that. Especially one as beautiful as this one.

A voice suddenly says, "Ja! Kant' ulapha!"

The girl jumps. Her face a contortion of horror. The guy she's been standing with runs off and disappears around the corner before any of us can react. Now there's a burly guy in his place. He grabs the girl's elbow and starts shouting.

"Ubusy lapha labantu bakho, hii?"

I know what's coming. I want it to be different this time. I want to grab Mama's nduku inside the cooler box I'm sitting on. I want to stand up and tell him to leave her alone. I want to take out that nduku so I can beat him 'stoo good!' like mama always promises to do to the neighbourhood drunks when they start getting rowdy near her stall.

Instead I sit there just the same way I did all those years ago and watch helplessly.

She tries to pull away from him.

"Sphila, mana," she begs, "mana shuwa!"

"Mana mana yani lapha wen' ung'wulel' ebantwini? Hii?"

He's almost frothing at the mouth. The girl's eyes are wide with fear and tears spill down her cheeks.

She whispers, "Sphila, mana ngiyakucel-"

The slap thunders so loud I wince. The girl's mouth is wide open. She touches her cheek with her right hand and stares at Sphila.

"Namhl' uzangibona," he says, and then slaps her again.

I sit and watch as he pulls her away by the elbow. He continues to shout and gesticulate wildly with his free hand as they walk away.

It’s dark.

Someone is praying.

I wish I could see her face.

I wish I could see something!

But it’s dark.

*

I've just finished writing my final paper at NUST. Some guys from my class bought a couple of bottles of Russian Bear to celebrate. One of the girls, Hlengiwe, joined us for the celebration. We're now sitting in Sipho's rented room in Selbourne Park. We're done with the first bottle of Vodka and the second one is pretty far in now. Hlengiwe is drunk as hell.

There isn't much in the room. A bed, a table, a single plate stove and two black Kango pots.

I remember that night. I want to tell Hlengiwe to leave but my mouth won't obey. She's been drinking like it's the end of the world and I know what happens (happened?) to her tonight.

I WANT IT TO STOP.

But it doesn't.

She asks me to walk her outside, just like she did the first time. I do. She wants to use the loo so I stand guard at the door while she goes in. I don't know why she asked me. She could have asked anyone.

When she comes out she's in a bad way. She's in tears and can barely stand up. I'm about to say the words I wish I never said to her. I want to stop myself but in that too, I'm helpless.

"You need to lie down," I say, "let's go back in the house."

The wheels are already in motion. We step into the house and she collapses onto the bed. Sipho casts her a cursory glance and the conversation continues. The rest of us are still strong enough to drink. So we drink. Sometime later Sipho shakes Hlengiwe and she does not respond. He shakes her again and there is no response. He squeezes her bottom. No response. Then he grins. A crooked grin that never leaves my mind even up to now.

"Madoda," he says, "nans' imbumb' yamahara."

There are four of us in the room. No one leaves. No one protests.

Thankfully the light returns before I relive my darkest secret.

*

When I open my eyes, Nyasha is sitting by my bedside. I watch her for a minute. She's wearing the same outfit from the club and a Chicago Bulls cap. In her hand is a beaten-up copy of *You*.

I try to sit up but my belly hurts way too much. I try to say something but instead I choke on my saliva and have a violent coughing fit. She bolts out of the room screaming for a 'fucking nurse.' She returns a few seconds later, looking like she just discovered a borehole in the middle of the Kalahari.

"I didn't think you were coming back, Mr."

"Well," I croak, "you and I have unfinished business."

"Lema!" she says, smiling, "I can't believe you're still thinking about that after the night you put us through!"

"Boys will be boys." I say.

She doesn't say anything.

"I think I actually saw my life flashing before my eyes," I tell her, "Not a good experience at all."

"Why? What did you see?"

"I'd rather focus on you, and those lips of yours."

She smiles and for the first time I see some shyness in her eyes. She looks down for a few seconds, then she looks at me and speaks up.

"I'm glad you woke up," she says, "I had so much fun with you last night."

"Really?"

"Yes, really. And I was worried I wouldn't get to do this again."

She kisses me.

ACKNOWLEDGMENTS

The list of people to thank for the production of this book is endless. My wife's hard to swallow but honest insights helped me a lot during the development of this work. I am indebted to Philani A Nyoni and John Eppel for their mentorship and never-ending encouragement to keep writing. My dear friend Noluthando Leonorah is brutal with her critique but she helps me stay realistic about my work and I am forever grateful for that, and for the wonderful review she wrote on Amazon to promote the book. If you read the back of the book before you bought or borrowed it then you have her to thank! Danny Rodrigues has to put up with a lot of crazy requests for art from me and I am so grateful to him for producing this beautiful cover.

My deepest thanks go to my parents and my siblings. They never stopped encouraging my reading habit and without that I would never have dared to become a writer.

ABOUT THE AUTHOR

Leroy Mthulisi Ndlovu

Leroy Mthulisi Ndlovu is a writer born and raised in Bulawayo, Zimbabwe. He loves to read and to write stories. He has a degree in Computer Science but writing is his first love.

He has published in a local newspaper, as well as online. He is also an amateur actor, having featured in Jane the Ghost and Golddiggers. Sirens is his first book.

www.ingramcontent.com/pod-product-compliance
Ingram Content Group UK Ltd.
Pitfield, Milton Keynes, MK11 3LW, UK
UKHW041639190726
13854UKWH00006B/2592

9 780620 899819